Pleasure and hunger ignite when a vampire tempts a dhampir with everything she desires. Can she resist the forbidden lust or will she surrender?

Layla, a twenty-one-year-old half-breed known as a dhampir, is incredibly beautiful and deadly. She drinks vampire blood for power and to stop the burning hunger.

The vampire academy is a hundred acres of land surrounded by high tech security to ensure that none enters or leaves. She is in the protection.

When she has lessons with the vampires, she struggles with her hunger and has to learn to trust them—a big issue for Layla because of her past, something she can neither forget nor run from. The past that haunts her dreams reminds her that she cannot hide as she lives her life in the academy.

Then there is Shade—an impossibly handsome vampire and Layla's one-on-one instructor. Desires she never knew rise whenever he looks at her. She cannot stop how her body reacts to his touch or how much she wants his body and his blood.

It is a forbidden lust that they share, one they must keep a secret from those around them or Layla risks everyone finding out who she really is.

Someone wants her dead. Layla's goals, deal with the vampires who hate dhampir's and keep herself alive. Can she do it?

Eternal Darkness
Copyright © 2012 Natalie Hancock
ISBN: 978-1-77111-292-5
Cover art by Martine Jardin

Published by eXtasy Books
Look for us online at:
www.eXtasybooks.com

Eternal Darkness
Cursed in Darkness Book One

By

Natalie Hancock

*My boyfriend Reece, who never gave up on my book,
even when I did.*

Prologue

His touch was like fire that burned into my soul. It branded me and made me feel pleasure I had never felt before as I arched under the searing touch of his fingers when they skimmed over my tight nipples. I almost growled at the feelings, I had no control over them at all it seemed. His fingers trailed down my stomach, leaving a tingling sensation of heat as he moved lower and lower. His soft lips touched my skin gently, below my breasts, making my breath hitch and my loins clench.

"We need to go." I moaned. The pleasure I was feeling was strong, but I could not ignore the fear. Fear that they would find me and kill me.

"I know."

He breathed onto my skin as his soft lips trailed kisses up my breast, to my nipple. He licked the hard bud before sucking on it. I moaned as desire shot though me, and I felt my legs open while large hands cupped the cheeks of my backside. I groaned and ran my fingers through his soft hair as he worried both of my nipples and sucked on them hard, turning the soft pink skin into dark pink. I cried out at the sensation as pain laced with the pleasure shooting through me.

He stopped, his lips sliding down my body once more until he was pressing little kisses on the inside of my thigh. I watched him do so, pleasure coursing through me along with a little fascination. He licked me, leaving a trail of heat before his tongue plunged deeply inside me. I moaned, my head falling back when he slid his tongue up over my clitoris. My legs went weak but he didn't let me fall, he just simply shifted, putting my legs over his shoulders and resumed pleasuring me.

"Please..." I moaned, needing more, *wanting* more as I pressed his face closer to me. He shifted and dropped one of my legs, but kept the other over his shoulder, which opened me wider to his touch. He bowed his head and his tongue snaked out to lick my clitoris again as he slid a finger into me slowly and easily. I growled loudly, the sound echoed around the room. The pleasure in the pit of my stomach grew, burning me, bringing me closer to ecstasy as he slid his finger out and then back in before adding another one at the same time. I felt myself clenching around his fingers, close to exploding, when he stopped. I growled, unable to help myself.

"Be still," his voice commanded while his free hand gripped my hip tightly. I squirmed, only a little, but did as he said, hoping he would do something, anything, to reignite the fire deep inside me. His fingers were unmoving inside me and I struggled not to move myself up and down on them. My heart was thumping rapidly in my chest and I could feel his matching the beat of mine on my thigh. He put his lips around my clitoris, his tongue gently running over it, making me clench a little before he sucked.

I exploded in white-hot pleasure and suddenly I was screaming and gripping him tight, trying to get away, but trying to move closer at the same time. His grip tightened on my hips as I squirmed and clenched my thighs together. He stopped sucking, but kept his fingers moving in and out of me and rubbed his thumb over my throbbing clitoris, which made my orgasm continuous. I no longer had any control over my body as I continued to scream, clutching his hard body as he pressed his face into my stomach, pushing me into the wall. I burned and ached, longing for him to be inside me. He kissed my hip as he moved faster, causing me to arch away from the wall and my screams to lock in my throat as I grabbed his shoulders and squeezed. I didn't care if I hurt him or not.

His hand moved from my hip to my breast where he squeezed gently, worrying my nipple in between his thumb and finger. I cried out, lost in the pleasure coursing through me. He stood, sliding his finger out of me and rubbing his hard muscled bare chest against my own, stirring the pleasure inside once more, even as I was trying to get my breath back and stop my heart from exploding out of my chest.

He opened my legs with his own and I heard him groan as I kissed his chest, my heavy breathing played across the beads of sweat dotting his skin. I ran my hands up his arms, feeling the muscles roll wherever I touched.

"I need you," I growled the words against his skin as I pulled on the back of his neck, bringing him closer to me. He growled when his erection encountered my wet heated flesh. His hands roamed over my chest, taking in the full mounds of my breasts and squeezing my hard nipples before he moved lower, his hands moving down my back and down the backs of my thighs before he gripped me and lifted me up easily. He tipped me back slightly against the wall, lifted my legs over both of his shoulders and then rubbed his erection against my clitoris. I moaned, unable to stop myself from arching away from the wall, putting my breasts close to his face.

"Look at me."

I didn't, I kept my eyes firmly shut, I knew that they would shut automatically when he entered me and filled me with pleasure—*more* pleasure than what I felt now. It seemed his touch alone could do the trick.

"Please..." I growled with pleasure, the sound vibrating from deep in my throat as he rubbed against me again.

"I want to look at you when you come," he said breathlessly.

My eyes opened at his words. My eyes locked onto his full lips as he smiled, showing me white teeth and sharp fangs. Pleasure shot through me and I moaned. The door to the room we were in burst open and many tall and strongly built men rushed into the room, their weapons drawn and aimed at the two of us.

I dropped to my feet, crouched low and hissed as the faceless men advanced on us both. I took his hand as he kicked out his leg twice, knocking the two closest men into the others. He ran and pulled me with him, out of the room and down the hall. The exit was not far from here. I knew that because we were so close when men came through the door, forcing us to hide and then discover that when we touched, we couldn't stop.

I heard the men advancing behind us and a new sudden burst of speed shot through me, making me run faster and take the lead. I reached out for the door when someone knocked me into the wall and pinned me there. I screamed, hissed and tried to bite the person, but he just punched me hard and knocked me to the ground.

"Let her go! You don't need her! Use me!"

Someone punched him and knocked him to the floor before another one kicked him, making him gasp in pain and cough. Someone grabbed my hair, pulled me to my feet and wrapped long fingers around my throat.

"Did you think you could escape from me?" the male hissed in my ear. "You will regret this, I can guarantee that." He pushed me into someone else, who started to drag me away.

"No, Dad! Let her go!"

"Help me!" I screamed as I fought against the hold on me and tried to get away and get to *him*. He could help me, I knew he could. We both knew he could.

"Get them away from each other!" someone yelled.

I tripped over my own feet and fell. The man holding me fell also and pinned me to the floor when I struggled and crawled along the floor.

"Get off me!" I screamed as I reached out once more. Our fingers touched and a tingling sensation shot through me just as the man holding me dragged me away. I screamed again and this time scratched the floor.

Our eyes met and I could see the promise in his eyes, a promise that we will see each other again. I kept my eyes locked with his and remembered them. Remembered everything, remembered him…

Chapter One

I hit the floor hard and groaned with both pain and annoyance. Pain because it was Father who knocked me to the floor, annoyance because it was the twelfth time he had done so, and easily.

"That was sloppy, daughter!" Father boomed, making his voice echo off the walls in the large room.

"You could at least go easy, you aren't exactly easy to knock down." I grumbled as I got to my feet. Nikalye watched me do so, wanting to help, but knowing he couldn't because Father would not allow it.

"Then what will you learn?" Logic, Father was all about it.

Then again, I supposed I was also. I stretched, trying to ease my aching muscles that were screaming for me to stop before I walked forward, facing Father, who was calm and not even sweating. He stood still without his fists in the air while he looked at me, checking me over. I was standing so in his eyes, I was fine.

He moved quickly. I was on the floor before I could even feel the pain of his punch. I didn't stay down, despite my need to breathe. I jumped to my feet, moved to the side to avoid another punch and twisted around. I kicked him in the back and he stumbled forward. Surprise was on my side so I easily knocked him to the floor when I hooked my leg around his and pushed him. I moved back quickly, knowing Father wouldn't stay down easily. He flipped himself to his feet and was on me in a second, knocking me to the floor with a sweep of his long legs. I rolled backward onto my hands and managed to kick him in the face before I back flipped, kicking him again and then jumped forward. My knees landed on his stomach and I knocked him down and put my hands, one on top of each other, over his heart.

"Dead," I breathed, fighting the pain in my ribs and legs. Father laughed and climbed to his feet easily, taking me with him before me put me on the floor.

"Well done, daughter."

I smiled weakly, not feeling all that victorious, when my body began to heat up quickly, spreading from my lower back where Nikalye's hands were, around to my stomach and up my rib cage.

"Broken ribs, but no punctured lung, thankfully," he muttered before he moved, taking my hand. Doxiak took Nikalye's place, placing his hands across my ribs just under my breasts. My body, having just cooled down from Nikalye's touch, flared white-hot and I hissed with pain as my ribs shifted and mended.

"You can take your ribs being broken, but not being mended?" he asked, his deep voice vibrating from his hands and through my body.

"Let me break your ribs and then you mend them." I growled. Nikalye squeezed my hand as Father laughed.

"Like father, like daughter," Doxiak mumbled, which caused me to smile...

I looked away from my window, from the view of the forests and the mountains in the distance and the stars in the dark sky that had just begun to fade with the rising sun. I sighed as my heart hammered painfully in my chest at the memory of me training with Nikalye and Father. I remembered it clearly, as if it had only happened yesterday instead of seven years ago. I always remembered everything taught to me, it was the only thing keeping me alive.

Father usually never fought with me, always let Nikalye be the teacher while he chose to sit and watch, making comments and telling me easier ways of doing something. I always enjoyed fighting Nikalye. I did learn a lot from him, except one thing, pain. Pain that I felt when someone hit me hard or the pain of me hitting someone and doing it wrong—that Nikalye refused to teach me because of the kind of vampire he was. Father understood and it was why he taught me.

I remembered being nervous. At fourteen, I was not exactly big, especially compared to Father, to anyone really. When Father hit you, you felt it shake every bone in your body.

I sighed again and looked around my room. After two years, it did not look any different. Just like everything else. Even the days were the same, dark.

A large canopy covered half of the hundred acres of land we lived in, blocking out the sun from above only because everyone needed protection from it. Such made it eternal darkness within the academy. We could still feel the heat and we could feel the cold wind, but the sun could not shine through the canopy.

I was in the accommodation building, a tall building with ten floors, each containing ten bedrooms. The bottom floor was large area full of settees, chairs, TVs and such. It had a separate room with toilets. The adults called it a common room. There was another building connected behind, which was where everyone ate and got their blood of course.

This academy was full of teenage vampires, all learning and training for the same thing. To survive.

Father thought it would have been best if I did not share a floor with the rest so I had the top floor, for privacy and for myself. The top floor only had two rooms, a bedroom and a bathroom. I had my own lift to get to this floor and I was the only one that knew the password, other than my guard, Nikalye and Father of course.

Unlike the other bedrooms, my room had a wall made entirely out of glass, which showed outside. It looked better when the sun was high. I had thick, black curtains because even though I liked the sun and the warmth in the morning, I did like it to be dark when I was sleeping.

My room was large and elegant. The carpet was thick, soft and black, at my request. The walls were red with black swirls up the side of every corner and part of the ceiling. I had a round red chair that sat in front of the large window. It was big enough to fit three people.

I had a four-poster king-sized bed, hand carved of dark mahogany wood with intricate swirls around the top of the headboard. There was a large chest, made from the same wood as my bed, set at the end and lined with thick silver. There was no lock. I did not worry, no one would be able to get in.

My walk-in wardrobe was in the wall at the end of my room. Just like my chest, no one could get into my wardrobe because at first glance there was nothing there.

On one inside wall was a large mirror and everywhere else was clothes. I had no love for clothes, even though I had lots. My only love was for my weapons. I fought to get them, fought to have them with me and would fight to keep it that way.

Before everyone started calling this place an academy, the buildings, built centuries ago on one hundred acres of land, housed the important vampires for their own safety while others went to war. They could sleep, eat in a large dining hall and have all the luxuries asked for.

Sadly, it appeared that such was not going to protect those inside for those who went out never came back, fights broke out and people died.

When our enemies became stronger, had better equipment—quick enough to kill us faster than being blown up—the fights within the land stopped. Everyone eventually agreed that in order to keep the number of their people up, they had to work together.

Almost everyone added more protection, growing more tall and thick trees within the land and wiring such with sensory cameras. A large canopy grew, protecting everyone from any sky attacks and the sun. Holograms placed around the outside of the boundaries hid our location and gave us more safety than we could imagine. No one had to worry about any of our enemies getting in.

It just meant that the place was thrown into darkness twenty-four seven. The others knew the risk and were not stupid. Although missing the sun while living here, they were vampires and it was in their nature not to go into the light.

Even though most didn't know where the academy lay and were aware of the added protection, the enemies didn't stop. They went for the children. At times babies were found brutally murdered, devoid of blood and sometimes limbs. Everyone came together and decided that all teenage vampires should have a chance at surviving. They built another two buildings, one to train in and another so everyone could sleep in their own rooms because they were not allowed into the mansion with the adults. Then began teaching all they needed to know about the enemy and how to survive.

I rubbed a hand across my face, climbed off my chair and walked across the room. Clad only in a short nightdress and barefoot, I opened my door and stepped into a large hallway where my lift waited. My bathroom was on the right. I took the lift to the ground floor.

I was thankful no one was in the common room when my lift opened. No one knew I was here, though everyone knew someone was because the men who created the lift to my room could not hide what they were doing.

The common room, with light walls and hard floors, was

longer than it was wide, and able to easily hold over two hundred. The settees and chairs were an assortment of colours, brightening the room. The walls had thick framed pictures of the most important people. The TVs—all ten of them—were large. There were shelves on one side of the wall filled with books and small cabinets filled with games, DVDs and music.

There were five lifts—not including my own—each one going to two floors a piece.

Just like my bedroom, tinted glass made up one of the walls looking out across the large area of grass, trees and the training building in the distance. Everyone could see out, but no one could see in. It was for privacy I was told.

I crossed the room and stepped into the *night*. Walking across the cold grass, I ignored the fact it was slightly tickling my bare feet. There were lights on the outside of each building that lit the space in-between. The training building was large and old, looking more like a medieval castle, more than somewhere where you would fight and learn.

I walked to the left of it, going through the trees. There was no light here, but that did not bother me. I was not afraid of the dark, nor did the dirt, leaves, stones and twigs that covered the ground underneath my feet bother me.

It was impossible to walk through these trees quietly, so when I heard the rustle of leather, the crunch of leaves and the snap of twigs, I sighed as I quickened my pace, stepping over a low branch and knowing the person following me would pick up speed also. I walked behind a large tree and ran forward to another quickly. When I got to it, I ran up the trunk and jumped high, grabbing hold of a branch. I swung around it, held myself straight with my hands before I quietly put my feet down onto the branch.

I looked behind me and saw him walk to the tree I was in

and then stop. He looked left and right and then turned into a full circle, scanning. When he was facing the trunk, I dropped to the floor, landing behind him, and grabbed both of his arms and pushed him into the tree, hard. He did nothing to defend himself.

"*Mi Belleza Oscura—*"

When I heard the meaning of my name in Spanish—*Dark Beauty*—I let him turn so he could look at me.

"You should know better than to sneak up on me, Nikalye," I said. He smiled, which made his handsome face more handsome. His long honey blond hair blew gently in the breeze as he looked at me.

"What are you doing out here? You know you are not meant to be alone at this time."

You would think that after two years of leaving Nikalye's accommodations, we would both be used to not seeing much of each other though he was never far away and always there when I needed him. It wasn't that simple, not after those years…

I swallowed the memory.

"I am fine." I said truthfully. Nikalye looked into my eyes for a couple of seconds before speaking.

"You do not feel hungry?"

"I will always feel hungry, Nikalye. You of all people know this." The mention of hunger brought a slight burning in my stomach, one that I ignored.

"That is true. You do not feel out of control?"

"No," I replied. Then I turned away from him, heading back through the trees. He followed. "I just wanted some air." This was only partially the truth. I was in control of myself. That was true, but I did not just need to get some air. I needed to shake off the memories.

"So you walked through the trees in just your lingerie?" Nikalye asked with amusement. He was used to the way I dressed and had never commented. He would not start now.

"I was just walking," I replied as I walked out of the trees. I heard voices so I stopped at the edge with Nikalye standing close behind me, comforting me without needing to try.

"*Mi, Belleza Oscura*, they will not harm you."

"I do not wish to be seen just yet," I told him. The voices were louder now and I heard laughter and cheering. I watched a group of teenagers come out of the building in front of me and walk across the path to the living accommodations. A male opened the door and held it so the others could pass him. He was the authority of the group, a tutor maybe? I could hear them as they thanked him and I could see him smile at them all. Everyone was friends with each other.

I sighed and as I did so, the male lifted his gaze up and met mine. I could see clearly that he was muscular, his blue top straining against his chest and arms. His hair was long and layered, the colour of the night, reaching past his shoulders like raven feathers. He had a perfectly sculptured face with a strong jaw line and full lips. His skin, I could see it from here, was smooth and flawless, white like pearls.

I did not look away from him. I couldn't explain it, I felt drawn to him. I felt connected.

"*Mi, Belleza Oscura*, what is wrong?" Nikalye asked.

I turned to look at him as he glanced over my shoulder. I opened my mouth and looked around, too, to explain how I had felt, but saw no one there.

"Nothing," I said instead and turned back to him. Once again, Nikalye looked at me before he offered me his hand.

"Come, I have clothes. I think it is time for you to meet Diaxon."

"Already?" I asked. This was the day I had been dreading. Meeting Diaxon meant that it was time for me to join in the lessons he and others taught. I would be around other vampires and that was what I was afraid of most.

"You will be fine, *mi Belleza Oscura,*" Nikalye said, reading my worries.

I nodded and held his hand tightly. I was not afraid of meeting anyone I had not met before.

I was afraid I would hurt them.

Chapter Two

We walked through the double doors to the training building into an entrance hall with just two doors. The walls were very bare here, painted white over the large rough stones. We headed across the large room, Nikalye's boots echoed off the floor and walls. He pushed open the door opposite the one we came in, and stepped to the side so I could walk through. The room was long with a high ceiling. The walls were black, making the green and red targets around the room stand out. I looked around and saw, much to my pleasure, weapons. All different kinds, throwing knives, short and long swords, sticks of bamboo and metal, spears and pikes, hung from the wall on the left side of the room.

Once again, there were only two doors in this room, one of which I was standing in and another on the other side.

"*Mi Belleza Oscura.*"

I looked at him. He handed me a pair of leather trousers and a black vest top before he turned his back as I pulled off my night dress and pulled on the vest. Once I had on my leather trousers, Nikalye turned around and took my nightdress.

"I must take my leave," he said a little sadly.

"*Guerrero*—"

He smiled, took my hand and squeezed it reassuringly. He knew what I feared. "You have not called me Warrior in a long time, *mi Belleza Oscura.* I have missed it."

I smiled slightly. "Stay with me."

"I will come back soon. You have my word."

With a sigh, I nodded. He stroked my cheek, kissed my hand and then left. I watched him go before I looked back into the room. I could smell the others, male and female. Sweat, adrenaline and determination. All of it smelled like something sweet. No one in this room was angered at all. Everyone was having fun, talking, laughing and fighting.

"Layla?"

I turned around and looked at the tall man striding down the hall toward me. He had shoulder length black hair, high cheekbones and full lips.

"Hello," I was polite as ever.

He smiled. "I am Diaxon, your training instructor and protector."

I bowed my head respectfully.

"What I would like you to do now, because I do not know how well you fight, is a trial run—if that is okay with you?"

"That is fine," I told him.

"The trial run is going to show me how well you fight when faced with danger. It will be testing you on your speed, strength, agility and cunning. At the end, I will be able to determine which group you will be joining, though I think I know which one I will be putting you in."

"Okay."

"Now, I know who you are and I have no doubt that you are an incredible fighter. Though you are twenty-one, you have not been taught here and your father wishes for you to be in the lessons, not assisting it."

"I understand."

"Very well. I will escort you there and then escort you back to your room."

I followed Diaxon across the hall to the opposite door. He

opened the door and held it so I could walk past him, then he led me down another hall, past some stairs and more doors to a door on the end.

He spoke as we walked in. "You will not see me, but I am in the room with you. Good luck." With that, he disappeared, literally.

This room was very similar to the other hall except there were no targets and weapons on the wall.

I glanced behind me and saw that there was also no door, no escape.

The lights on the high ceiling flickered and I looked at them as they went out. The darkness was so thick, I could not see through it. I took a deep breath, closed my eyes to concentrate and took a step forward.

I ducked the fist that would have slammed into the side of my face and swept my foot out. I stood back up and bent backward to avoid a leg and grabbed the next one that came. I pulled it toward me, using the attacker's surprise against him. I knocked him into the floor as the lights flickered on. I took a step back and watched as the man disappeared. I looked around. No one was in the hall with me now, but that did not mean there wasn't anyone there. I stayed still as stone and closed my eyes once more. My senses told me there were two coming from the right side, one creeping up behind me and one coming from above.

I opened my eyes as the one above me dropped. I turned to the side, avoiding his body, and closed my fingers around his thick muscled throat. I slammed him to the floor like the other one, before I twisted around and grabbed an arm. I twisted around his body until we were back to back and then jumped up, lifting myself up and kicking a man in front of me with both of my feet before I jumped up again and rolled backward over his back. I wrapped my arm around his neck and slammed him into the floor. I rolled backward and crouched low, but nothing attacked me.

The lights flickered, going off and on quickly. I let out a quiet breath and straightened when the ground rumbled. I jumped backward as a large beam shot out of the floor. I sensed someone behind me and quickly jumped up high. I grabbed hold of the beam while it was still moving and twisted around like a gymnast when it stopped. I balanced myself on top and looked down. I saw that it wasn't just someone, it was six someones, all big males wearing black. I stood carefully and placed my right foot in front of my left. The men below me looked up before one jumped. He landed on the beam without a wobble and walked toward me.

I bent my knees slightly when the man stopped. He was close enough to touch. When he twisted around on one leg, his other leg turned in a high arc that aimed for my head. I ducked, but he swept my legs out from underneath me and I slipped off the beam. I grabbed hold of it, swung around and kicked the man in the face before I balanced myself on my hands and then onto my feet. I did not watch the man fall, but jumped into the air and back flipped over a man behind me. I wrapped my legs around his neck and turned my body to the side as I fell. I grabbed the beam as the man twisted around at an odd angle and lost his balance. I let go of him when I was upside down and the man toppled off the beam. I slowly put my feet down before I back flipped off it. I landed on the floor silently and stayed crouched.

The men come at me at the same time. One man threw his fist toward my face. I side stepped it and his punch landed in the face of another man so hard, he flew across the hall. I then dodged someone's kick and it landed in someone else's stomach. I took a couple of steps back as two vampires swept their hands out, their intent was to grab me. Instead, they grabbed the necks of each other. I ran up them and while airborne, kicked them both in the face, one after the other. I landed on my feet and backed flipped quickly as the last man left twirled a bamboo stick.

We circled each other and then he hit out with the stick fast. I dodged it, but he hit out with the other side and pain flared through me. I didn't react, but grabbed the stick before he could swing it back. He pulled on it hard. I dropped to the floor and skidded between his legs. I grabbed both of them and pulled hard. He fell forward. I jumped on his back and stuck one of my knees in his neck. He grunted with pain, but lay motionless when I pressed the pressure points on his neck.

I slowly got to my feet as the lights went off again. I knew someone had appeared in the room with me. I just couldn't tell where. I breathed in deeply and closed my eyes. The man walked toward me slowly and made no sound. Keeping my eyes shut, I moved forward quickly and hit him in the face, making his head snap back in surprise. He looked around, but I dropped to the floor and knocked his feet from under him. I kicked him as he fell. He flew across the hall and smashed into the wall opposite. He slumped to the floor and didn't get back up.

I opened my eyes and saw the lights were on. I also saw the door open and a man walked in with two spears, one was black, the other red. I watched as he walked toward me and stopped. He held the red spear out. I took it from him as he spoke.

"Watch, listen and concentrate." Then he swung his spear fast.

I put mine up to block it and swung the other end, but he blocked that.

He smiled at me. "Good. Move your body with the stick, don't be afraid of using all of your strength, you won't hurt me."

I nodded and turned my body to the side. I bent my knees

slightly and held one hand in the middle of the first part and the other in the middle of the top part. The man seemed to approve because he took the same stance. He stood like stone and when I hit with my stick, he lifted his to block it, but I pulled back at the last second and sent the bottom of the stick into his stomach.

He doubled over and I hit him in the face, twisted the stick in my hands, and hit him in the stomach again while I kicked his feet and knocked him to the floor. I jumped on him and aimed the point toward his neck. He knocked it away from me and used his stick to push me off. He swung and I ducked, then back flipped as he used it to try and knock my feet from under it. I swung my stick, knocked his out of his hands and then jumped on him again. He fell to the floor and I put the sharp end to his neck.

"My dear, you are an extraordinary fighter."

I climbed off him.

He got to his feet and bowed. "It has been an honour." He turned and walked away with both sticks.

"Well done, Layla. Please, come this way," Diaxon said as he held the door open. We walked down the corridor and into the other hall. "You did very well. Your father will be pleased."

"Thank you." I looked around the room once more.

"You remind me of your father, the way you move."

I smiled at that compliment, liking it very much. Diaxon opened the doors again and then followed me into the hall.

"You are the first in a long time to complete that trial," he said as we walked along the hall. A female taller than me with very long chocolate brown hair twisted to one side of her head looked at me curiously. Maybe it was my looks. Maybe it was just because she had never seen me here before.

"Master Diaxon," she bowed her head respectfully.

"Mireuves, if you will wait here, I shall be back shortly."

She nodded and looked at me once more and I at her. She had a heart shaped face, big blue eyes and full shiny lips. Her knee length dress hugged her body and showed off her curves. She caught me looking and smiled lightly before I turned away and walked outside. Diaxon and I did not speak as we walked toward the living accommodation building.

"Everyone is taught five different things in total, three of those you will have with me and you will have them every day of the week. One is learning about how the enemy thinks and fights, uses their weapons and how you should fight. Another is practical hand-to-hand combat and finally a practical weapon combat, taught with simple weapons. Once every three days, you will have a lesson with Reikez, of which I will assist so if you should need me I will be there. At the end of every week, you will have your normal lessons mixed into one in the morning, and in the afternoon. You will have a session with Kharlo, he teaches about more advanced weapons.

"I am not going to be teaching you during your fighting sessions, my assistant, Shade, will be. He will be with you for each of your lessons so he can have one-on-one time with you if you are too advanced, and if you are too advanced in non-combat lessons, then you may watch."

I nodded.

"Now, you will have a lot of free time because everyone gets an hour to eat after each lesson, an hour before fighting and two hours after fighting, and you have two hours of free time in which to catch up with your friends, but I am free whenever you need me, whether I am in lessons or assisting." He pulled out a gold pocket watch and looked at the time.

"Okay, that is all. Master Nikalye or I will find you to let you know when your first lesson is."

I nodded.

"I will see you soon." He smiled and turned to walk away.

I watched him go and suddenly felt alone. I thought about going out of the boundaries. I could do so easily, but my father would be incredibly mad. It was something I had seen many times and did not wish to be on the receiving end of.

I needed to do something.

Already I felt as though someone was watching me.

That was never a good thing.

I looked around and made sure there was no one around and no one in the trees before I crossed the grass between the training building and the living accommodations.

The feeling of someone watching me was stronger out here. I just didn't know who it could be or where they could be. The air pulsed against my skin and made the hairs on the back of my neck and arms stand on end.

I looked around me before I walked to the right to a large clump of trees. I walked along the line of trees, past the training building and into an even darker part. Something cold passed over me. My hair stood on end and my skin broke out in goose bumps. I stopped and stayed still as stone. I sensed no one around me, but once again, the feeling of someone watching me was there.

"You're not safe here."

The voice was a whisper behind me, but when I turned quickly, I saw no one there. I looked around slowly before I walked through the trees. Something glittered out of the side of my vision, a knife with a red handle and intricate swirls embedded from base to tip.

I shivered as something cold washed over me again. I rolled my head on my shoulders and looked at the knife again. It was a beautiful knife. I liked knives. I very much wanted this one.

I reached out to touch the handle. It was warm. I picked it up and looked at it closely before I turned it in my hand. I felt the blade, ran my finger along the swirls and felt the weight. The handle was smooth to the touch and the blade was cold. It felt so natural in my hands.

It also felt natural to turn the knife around so that the blade was pointing at my chest. I closed my eyes and let the feeling of anticipation wash over me. I grabbed the blade's handle with both of my hands, ready to push…

Chapter Three

The blade cut through my top and into my skin. My heart hammered in my chest and I distinctively heard someone chuckle.

"Layla?"

Hands grabbed me and pulled the knife away from my chest. I opened my eyes and hissed at the same time as he pushed me against a tree and slammed my hands above my head. I watched the knife fall to the floor, sinking into the soft ground easily.

I shivered and felt goose bumps break out on my skin. I looked at the man holding me against the tree. "Nikalye—"

"Are you okay?"

"I'm fine," I replied. He looked at me for a second before he let my hands go. I ignored the slight sting of my wrists as I looked around. I saw nothing. The feeling of someone watching me was gone.

"What happened?" Nikalye asked as he turned my face to look at him.

"I don't know." I looked around again before I looked at Nikalye and took his hand. "Did you see anything?"

He shook his head. "What made you venture out?"

"I felt as though I was being watched."

Nikalye nodded. "That is what I felt before I found you." He looked around. "Come, I will escort you back to your room." He held his arm out.

I bent to pick up the knife. Nikalye's hand closed around my wrist, but I didn't need to touch it for the scent and the presence of the owner to wash over me like air. I growled.

"What is it?" Nikalye asked as he looked around quickly, looked for the danger that was no longer here.

"Mother," I used Spanish. When I looked at him, he frowned.

He used the language as well. "That is not possible. She is dead."

"I do not know," I reverted to English and heaved out a sigh. "Maybe I am wrong." Though I had never been wrong before.

"Come, let's go." He pulled me to my feet and kept hold of my wrist as we walked. We didn't speak, but I noticed that Nikalye didn't watch where we were going, but was looking everywhere. That worried me.

"Nikalye," I pulled my wrist out of his grip and held his hand. "Speak to me." We stopped at the front of the doors. Nikalye looked around and then looked at me.

"You trust me, do you not?"

The Spanish again showed my trust. "Yes, of course."

The English returned. "I will be watching over you, *mi Belleza Oscura*, I will never be far." He kissed my forehead. "Trust me."

I closed my eyes as he hugged me and felt the wind as it blew my hair from my shoulders. I opened my eyes, but Nikalye was gone. I looked around toward the dark trees before I turned around and pushed the door open. I walked across the empty common room and into my lift, pressing the button to go up to my room.

I looked up as the door across the room opened and saw the tall male I had seen earlier step into the building with two males.

He looked in my direction and I looked at his handsome

features once more before I looked into his eyes. I saw the colour of them and recognition washed over me, but I didn't know why. Yes, I saw him earlier, but as I looked into his eyes, I knew I had never met this male before that. I definitely would have remembered, but I felt as though I had seen those bright silver eyes before—before I had come here.

I saw him tilt his head to the side and look at me with curiosity as my lift doors shut. I stared at the door with my mouth slightly open. It was very tempting to press the button to stop my lift, but after tonight, after what I had nearly done. The thought was not as tempting as it sounded.

Who was he though? Why did he seem so familiar to me?

Once upstairs, I showered. My bathroom was as large as my bedroom. It was lighter, the marble walls were white, the floor grey. There was a square hole in the floor to the left, large enough for me to swim in. It served as my bath. The walk in shower took up the entire wall on the right, separated by a shower wall made from squares of marble. There was toilet and sink in the middle, opposite the door.

I washed the dirt off my feet and the sweat from my body and instantly felt calm and relaxed once I was clean. I even curled my hair in loose curls—something I did not do normally—while I stood in my shorts and bra. Nikalye came into my room. He didn't bother knocking, just simply walked in. He knew when not to disturb me.

"*Mi Belleza Oscura*, how are you?"

"I am feeling better, thank you," I replied as I looked at my clothes.

"Diaxon wishes to introduce you to the class so you know who you are going to be with and who is going to be teaching you."

"Now?" I asked.

He nodded. "Obviously no one could get into your lift to

tell you," Nikalye explained.

"That explains it," I said with a nod as I pulled out a dress. It was a small black strapless gothic lace dress with a white belt under the bust and a full skirt, which came to the middle of my calves. I pulled on some black high heels with black ribbons criss-crossing my calves.

For the first time in seven years, I really looked at myself in the mirror. I had a curvy figure and a large chest so I filled my dress out perfectly. I showed a lot of leg. I had long and thick pitch-black hair and slightly tanned skin—thanks to my Egyptian heritage—a round face, big violet coloured eyes, small nose and full lips.

I looked past all that at my piercings. I had one of my eyebrows pierced, my nasal septum pierced, my lip pierced on both sides, the tops of my ears pierced and my tongue pierced. I also had my belly button and my nipples done—though no one would know about that one.

I sighed and looked away from my reflection and walked out of my wardrobe. Nikalye looked at me and smiled as I shut the door.

"You are a beauty, *mi Belleza Oscura.*"

"Thank you, Nikalye." He offered me his arm and I took it before we headed out. We got down to the common room and as soon as I had locked my lift, we were out in the warm darkness.

I could hear Diaxon speaking as we neared the training hall. I stopped at the door and took a deep breath before walking in.

Chapter Four

Diaxon was speaking to a tall, light brown haired, kind faced man, and he did not stop speaking to him as we walked in. I wondered if that was Shade. Somehow, I didn't think so. I looked at all the teenagers standing around on the left side of the hall while they talked in hushed voices, smiled and laughed with each other. There were more males than females in the group and they were all tall and very handsome. The females were also tall, but I had yet to meet one taller than the males. They were all very beautiful and perfect.

Then again, vampires were always perfect.

Once everyone noticed me, they all stared openly as I crossed the room to the corner with Nikalye behind me. I could shadow myself well, but I would be wasting my time. I let them look. They had not seen me here before and I knew they were just sizing up the competition. To everyone, I looked like I could be smashed.

I was not that delicate, no one could take me down easily.

They were all different to me. Where I had colour in my skin, everyone else was pale. Though legends said they are always pale because they were dead. They were not, they used their bodies as humans do. They could get hurt, they bled and they tired and needed to rest. They even needed to use the toilet.

Their hearts beat because they needed oxygen to travel

around their bodies, like any human. The blood carried oxygen and that was what vampires needed in order to survive because breathing was not enough. The oxygen they breathed just died. That was why they drank human blood, because the oxygen was already there.

It was a curse.

True, vampires could not go out in the sun, but that was because their skin was very sensitive. It was like having an allergic reaction, they would burn. They had never seen the sun, never been exposed to the sun's rays. That was why they were pale.

I was different of course, yes, I was a vampire, but I was also half-human, known as a *dhampir*. I shared what vampires had, strength, speed, keen senses and intelligence, but I could walk in the sun. I enjoyed the sun very much and was often in it. I did not have to worry about my smooth and flawless skin losing its colour.

Like all vampires, I was strong, but I did not get my strength from human blood. I had never touched a human for their blood — that was the main difference — I drank the blood of creatures that walked hidden among humans. I already had oxygen travelling through my blood system, oxygen that did not die when I breathed it in, so I had no need to take the sip of life from humans.

Vampire blood held power and that was why I drank vampire blood. Call me selfish, but either way if I did not drink for the power, I drank for the thirst. I did need to quench it somehow.

As for the other creatures of the night, werewolf blood had less power, a lot less than a demon. I did not plan to drink from a wolf any time soon — too many bad memories where that was concerned.

The blood of an angel held more power than that of a vampire, maybe it was because they were holy. I did not

know. I was not religious. I liked the taste of angel's blood —
I had tasted many, enough that maybe I had become
addicted.

I would have to stick with vampire blood. The thought
made me hungry.

We ate normal food of course. We could not keep our
bodies strong with no nutrients and vitamins and such, no
matter how powerful we were. You could be the most
powerful vampire in the world, but if you did not eat, even
the weakest vampire with a good diet could kill you.

Our enemies had killed many of us because we had not
fed properly, and our enemies were human.

You would think that being a creature with extra strength
and stamina we would be able to take on the humans. It was
not that easy. The humans knew about the vampires and all
of the other creatures that walked the night.

They knew and had ways to kill us.

Though they did not kill us straight away, they captured
us first. They had their ways. They needed to be stopped
because they had our bodies restrained so we could not
attack them. They poked and prodded around inside us —
quite literally — they learned what we could do and they
took what was inside us, what made us powerful — our
blood — and they injected it into willing humans.

The experiments didn't go right. The humans grew
stronger and yes, they had keener senses and could even
walk out in sunlight, but their bodies changed. They grew
bigger, grew extra limbs and became monsters.

They were stronger than any other creature alive.

They were what everyone knew as Mutations.

Every creature, every vampire, werewolf, shifter, demon
and angel were hunted by these humans. We were being
killed more and more as the days went by. Already the
demons who wielded fire were extinct. I think the angels

would be next, there were so few already.

I turned my attention away from the curious vampires and sighed as I looked across the room, my thoughts still on the angels. It had been so long since I had seen an angel, though I did not make friends with them. I find that I lusted for their blood more than I wished to.

"Right," Diaxon called, having finished his conversation. "Now the reason you are all here, and as you are obviously aware, we have a new member to this academy. Her name is Layla and I expect you to show her how respectful you can be, especially because we have a guest with us today." He bowed his head to Nikalye before he caught everyone's eye and then looked at me and smiled. "This is the smallest class because these are the strongest and fastest and they do not need to be taught the basics, such as how to stand or hold your fist when you punch, like the others do." He turned away and looked at one of the female vampires. "Please, introduce yourself."

The female stepped forward and smiled, it was Mireuves. She had changed out of her dress and was now wearing flared black trousers and a thin-strapped dark blue top.

"I am Mireuves, as you know. I am eighteen years old, the youngest in this group. Though I have never been taught how to fight, I tend to use logic and think before I act, which is how I came to be in this group."

I nodded as she stepped back.

"I am Arezon," another female said and stepped forward. She was very tall, the tallest female it seemed, with very long dark honey coloured hair tied in a plait over one shoulder. She was very pretty with big brown eyes and thick lashes, a straight nose and slightly full lips. "I am twenty, the oldest female in the group," she and Mireuves exchanged a smile. "Because I am tall, it is hard to knock me down. I can lift my legs up very high." She demonstrated her point and lifted her right leg up straight. All of the males groaned and the females, including Arezon, sniggered.

"Kalitha," a tall female with shoulder length light golden blonde hair with a side fringe said in a casual manner. Half of her face was covered, but I could see her rosy pink cheek, full lips and a bright green eye.

"Kiuthil," a female with dark golden blonde hair in the exact same style as Kalitha, only the opposite side said, in an equally casual way. She had the same facial features.

"They are sisters by father," Nikalye murmured from behind me.

Explains, I murmured in my mind. I knew that Nikalye would be able to hear my words. I looked at them both and waited for more, but they kept quiet.

"Name's Lohron," a male said. I turned my attention to him and saw that he was looking me up and down slowly. He had short brown hair, tied to the bottom of his neck. His eyes were bright yellow. He was also not paying attention as he looked at me, so when a male next to him elbowed him hard and made him grunt, I turned my attention to him.

He had short burgundy coloured hair, dark green eyes, high cheekbones and full lips. He smiled widely, showing fangs, when he saw me looking at him with my head tilted to the side.

"Niaxoz," he said as he bowed his head. I smiled slightly and he widened his smile. "I am twenty years old, the same age as Lohron here. Kiuthil and Kalitha are both nineteen, just so you know." I nodded with a smile and he nodded in return before he continued. "I am good at fighting and, just like Arezon, *I* think before I act." He looked at Lohron as he said it and everyone laughed.

"Calm down please." Everyone did so quickly.

"I'm Teigan," a male spoke. I turned my attention away from the handsome Niaxoz and looked him up and down.

He was much more handsome to look at with white blonde hair and a very handsome face. He had a square jaw, full lips and black eyes, which stood out in contrast with his hair. "I, also, am twenty. I am good at fighting with any weapon, but using a nunchuck to fight is my weapon of choice."

I looked at him for a second longer before I turned my eyes to another male that stood next to him. He had long red hair, spiked on the top, high cheekbones, thin lips and slightly slanted eyes.

"Zhanju," he introduced. "I am nineteen and I am a black belt in martial arts." I raised my eyebrows at that. It was not every day you met a vampire who was a black belt in martial arts. He must be an incredible fighter.

"Make it quick please, I do have a lesson to teach in a couple of hours," Diaxon called out.

"Leidon," a long blonde haired male with sapphire blue eyes said, bowing his head slightly. "I am nineteen and like to use my speed on my side, which makes it hard to be knocked to the floor."

"Berlox," a large, dark brown haired male said in a deep voice. I raised my eyebrows as I looked at him. He was not as tall as the other males of this group, but he sure was the biggest, muscle wise. "I am nineteen—"

"And can knock someone to the floor with his stare," Lohron said loudly, which resulted in everyone laughing.

"I am Tianshuk." A tall male with light brown hair, tied to the back of his head and bright blue eyes smiled. "I am twenty years of age, and like Teigan, I enjoy fighting with weapons more than hand-to-hand."

"Gutax—"

"Eailek—" the two last males spoke at the same time. They both had long hair, curling around their long faces. Gutax had dark brown and Eailek has black. They both had the same bright green eyes except Eailek had one bright blue eye. I tilted my head to the side, looking at him. He smiled slightly as someone spoke.

"Only one of his eyes changed colour when he was born."

A shiver ran through me at the sound of his voice. My heart picked up speed and I felt the hairs on my arms and the back of my neck stand on end, not because of anything dangerous, but because the voice that spoke sent shivers of pleasure through my entire body. I looked at the male that had just walked into the room and could not stop. The sense of recognition came back as I looked into his silver eyes.

Chapter Five

His eyes, framed by thick lashes any female would love, looked at me with so much heat in them, it was a wonder I didn't fall to the floor with pleasure. He smiled and I stopped breathing altogether.

"We think it's because his mum cheated on his dad," Gutax's voice sounded faraway.

"Half and half, nothing wrong with that," Eailek said with a shrug.

"Layla, this is Shade, my assistant. Shade, this is Layla."

Shade bowed his head and kept his eyes on me. I let my gaze travel down him and couldn't help but wonder how magnificent he would look naked.

"Layla," he spoke in a low voice, which effectively, yet surprisingly, made my lips part slightly with pleasure. It was all I could do to stop myself from jumping him.

"Right, now I have a lesson to assist. If you," Diaxon turned his attention to Nikalye, "wouldn't mind continuing with the lesson we had earlier, just to get Layla on the right track so she knows what she is doing?"

"It will be my pleasure." Nikalye bowed his head.

Diaxon nodded and looked at everyone before he left.

I saw, but had not yet looked away from Shade, unable to help myself. When Nikalye gently touched my arm, I jumped and looked at him.

"You have the same look you had before, what is

wrong?" he asked in Spanish.

I shrugged and glanced at the others who were not paying us the slightest attention. "I do not know," I replied, knowing we'd keep to the same language.

"You will tell me once you know?"

I nodded and smiled. "Of course I will."

He nodded and turned to the others. Some were staring at us, having heard, but not understanding our conversation. Others were talking in quiet voices among each other.

"As you know, I am Nikalye. Most of you, if not all, already know me as a guard for Master Tyroz." Everyone said hi respectfully. He smiled at each one before speaking to me. "Now, they have already covered the basics. Who our enemies are, what they do and how long they have been doing it. If you are surrounded by a bunch of humans and you see no weapons, what will you do, Lohron?"

Lohron looked at Nikalye. "You fight them."

I shook my head even before he finished his sentence.

Nikalye chuckled softly. "Incorrect. Does anyone know?"

No one answered and I knew Nikalye was shaking his head behind me.

"Can you give everyone the right answer, Layla?"

I smiled slightly. He knew I could. I kept the Spanish up as I gave him the right answer.

"Yes, you try and get away from them," he translated so everyone else knew my answer. "But why don't you just, as Lohron says, fight them?"

I answered again in Spanish. While the others did not understand what I was saying, Nikalye could, and he was the only one I wanted to.

"Correct, the humans will kill you with whatever weapons they have with them," Nikalye said once more for the class.

"But he said you're surrounded by humans and you see

no weapons," Tianshuk said, his arms crossed over his muscular chest. His expression said he thought I was incredibly stupid, but couldn't help being turned on by the sight of me.

I replied in Spanish, and Nikalye translated. "If you are surrounded by humans, you can always guarantee that they have weapons and they are just hiding them, waiting for you to attack. What Layla said is correct, Tianshuk."

"Does she speak English?" Lohron asked.

"Yes, she does. She does not know whether she can trust you and this is why she is speaking Spanish," Nikalye answered.

I threw Lohron a grin.

"Now, if there is only one human and you see the human has a weapon, do would you do?"

"You run," Niaxoz answered.

"Why?"

"Because, just like the weapons, a human after a vampire is never alone. As soon as you attack, you'll be ambushed," he replied, obviously catching on to what I was saying.

"Very good. Yes, a human is never alone, just like they are never without weapons." Nikalye looked at everyone before speaking again. "You need to know this because nearly all of you are inexperienced. If I were to let you off the premises, you would not know what to do. You need to learn how to survive, you need to learn what others could not."

"What do you mean, nearly all of us are inexperienced?" Kiuthil asked.

"What I mean is, in the past three years, only two of you have completed the trial run. Some have gotten close, yes, but they were the only ones who knew the best and easiest ways to get through the obstacles instead of the hardest. Compared with all of you, they are more likely to be able to survive should they get attacked by humans —"

The door to the hall opened and a tall female vampire walked in. Her hair was in a high bun and she wore a tight skirt and shirt. Nikalye met her halfway and they had a quiet word. He nodded and, after saying something else to him, she walked away.

Nikalye faced me and bowed his head slightly before he left us alone. Once the door shut, everyone walked up to me, looking at me curiously, heatedly or jealously. Standing this close to them, I saw that I was the smallest, but not by much.

"What's with the guard?" Lohron asked.

I looked at him. The way he said it he was the leader of the group. I did not think the others thought of him that way.

"Ah, she's the silent type I see," Tianshuk said with a smirk, bringing my attention to him.

"She's the one that completed the trial," Mireuves spoke up as she looked at my appearance with curiosity. The others looked at me also, but their expressions were more of disbelief than curiosity.

"There's no way she completed the trial, no one has completed the trial since Shade," there was disbelief in Lohron's voice as he looked at Shade.

"She doesn't look strong." Gutax looked into my eyes. I did not think he meant that as an insult. I did not look strong.

"I could take her," Zhanju muttered, clearly meaning it as an insult.

"And what if she beats you? What if, instead of her being underneath you, you find yourself underneath her?" Shade asked from across the room, his eyes on me.

"I'll believe it when I see it," Lohron said smugly.

"*Idiota,*" I muttered as I turned my attention away from Shade to look at Lohron.

"Ooooooh," the others said, then laughed. They obviously

knew what idiot meant in Spanish.

"Watch it, this kitten has claws." Eailek laughed.

Lohron threw him and the others a dirty look before he smiled at me and showed his fangs. "So you think you can pin me then?"

I just smiled.

"Prove it, and we can make this fun. You can pick how we do it, hand-to-hand or weapons." He looked at my short dress. "And I think I might just enjoy putting a girl on the floor while wearing a dress that short."

I raised my eyebrows as Nikalye walked into the room. He looked at me, raising his eyebrows when he saw me surrounded. I just shrugged and walked back to the spot I was before, a small smile on my face.

"Sorry about that. We had some difficulties at the gates," Nikalye said, turning his attention to everyone else.

"What difficulties?" someone asked.

"It does not matter at this time." Nikalye turned his attention to me. "*Mi Belleza Oscura*, are you okay?" His Spanish was always flawless.

I knew he referred to what happened when he was absent. He missed nothing. I kept to Spanish. "I'm fine."

He nodded before turning to the quiet teens that were looking at both of us in awe. I knew Nikalye knew nothing had happened, he would have been able to see as well as get it from my mind. I was not hurt and that was the main thing.

"Okay, resuming with what I was saying to you, yes most of you are indeed inexperienced, but we can change that if you *listen*," with the last word, he raised his voice.

I looked over in time to see Lohron lean away from Berlox quickly.

"If you do not want to be here, Mr. Zaufen, then please leave."

Lohron did not move.

"What makes you think we can learn anything and be strong enough to go out of this place and survive?" Arezon asked quietly. Everyone turned to look at Nikalye.

"You have not been outside of these premises since you have been here, no?"

"None of us have," Niaxoz replied.

Nikalye glanced at me before looking away. He gazed at each vampire closely before speaking. "You are all very good fighters, there is no doubt about that, but if you go out there unprepared it is very likely that you will not survive, just as others before did and others before them. It is one thing learning about our enemies and how to fight, it is another thing actually doing it if you should get in that situation." He began to pace.

I was amazed at how much attention everyone was paying to him.

"If you were to all run at me now and attack, I can easily have you all on the floor within a second."

"Yeah but you're a guard for Master Tyroz," Tianshuk said.

Nikalye bowed his head. "Yes, I am, but that has nothing to do with it. If you attack me, it will be unplanned and you will not be working together. Unlike the humans who strategize, who work together to get what they want. When one of them dies, the others attack harder. This is what you need to be doing. If I should give you a chance to discuss how you will handle a situation, you stand more of a chance of hitting me."

"Is this why we have more fighting lessons than anything else?" Lohron asked.

"Yes, we can teach you about the enemies, but that alone is not enough. We can teach you how to use advanced weapons, and while long ranged is very much effective, again that is not enough. You need to learn how to fight so you can *run* if you are in the situation that calls for it. You may think that sounds cowardice, but it is the only way we can survive. Yes, we go out and we fight them occasionally, but only when they threaten us to the point where we have no choice." He glanced at me.

I nodded. I understood that when he had to go, he had to go. It was what he did, and I knew — we both knew — if I had a choice, I would be there by his side, fighting to keep my people safe and alive.

"Do you all understand?"

Everyone but me chorused yes.

"Now, let us talk about the enemy. They have very advanced weapons which can kill us instantly, or draw out our deaths in a very painful way. This is one example of where you will need to run. One of those ways is liquid silver in the bullets. When the bullet enters, it releases liquid silver into the bloodstream. Who can tell me what this does?"

"Kills you slowly?" Mireuves spoke up, speaking the most obvious answer.

"Indeed it will, but how? How does it kill you slowly?"

No one said a word and I was amazed with how little everyone knew. With a sigh, I closed my eyes and took a deep breath before speaking. "The silver is released into your bloodstream, burning you from the inside, killing your blood cells, starving you." It was a very horrible way to go.

"Good, yes," Nikalye said as everyone started to mutter to each other. "It is the most effective way to ensure the death of a vampire. They also have guns that shoot silver nets out. Now these nets have been specially weaved to render us immobile — "

I blocked out Nikalye's words. They stirred something ugly inside of me. Memories I wished to forget, but never would. I watched him move in front of the others, gesturing with his hands as he spoke. Everyone was watching him, paying close attention to his words, occasionally nodding to show they understood. They wanted to learn, there was no doubt about that, but they did not know how serious everything was until now.

I looked at Shade. I wondered if he already knew everything Nikalye was saying, just as I did. It would make sense for him to learn about this just as everyone else had. He would not be an assistant otherwise.

I glanced at the others. They were still watching and listening intently. It was obvious that they did not know this stuff.

A shiver ran down my spine, almost pleasantly. I looked away from the others to look back at Shade. He was looking at me fully now, taking in my appearance curiously.

"Okay, that is all for this session, if you will make your way out of the hall."

I looked away from Shade quickly and saw Nikalye walking over to me.

"I would like you all to remember what I have told you this session. It is very important." He held his hands out and I placed mine into his. He looked at me with concern, paying no one any attention now.

"I am fine, Nikalye," I said to ease his worries.

He nodded. "I know how you feel about all of this, but they must learn."

"And they will. Do not worry."

He nodded again and took my wrists in his hands. He ran his thumbs along the inside of my wrists, soothing the skin only he knew was sensitive. I turned my hand and placed it in his.

"*Mi Belleza Oscura —*"

"I promise you, Nikalye, I'm fine," I promised in Spanish. I saw the red in his eyes shift slightly before he nodded. He squeezed my hand and then pulled me across the room, past the others who had not moved and were obviously watching our exchange.

"You have not felt anything weird?" Nikalye asked once outside. We walked on the grass while the others followed the path.

"No, Nikalye," I glanced at him. "What happened?"

"*Mi Belleza Oscura*, Diaxon will let you know, at my request, if he wishes."

"Why not tell me now?" I asked. He stroked my cheek gently.

"We do not wish to worry you, *mi Belleza Oscura*. You have been through a lot."

I nodded and did not question him further. As we neared the other building, Nikalye slowed down. I knew he was not going to be coming to my room with me. I was a little disappointed.

"Thank you, Nikalye." He bowed and stopped near the door to kiss my hand.

"See you again soon, *mi Belleza Oscura*."

"I look forward to seeing you again soon, *Guerrero*." I smiled as I watched him walk away. I ignored everyone staring and whispering as they walked past me until Nikalye disappeared into the shadows.

Chapter Six

I could hear the others in the feeding hall, talking and laughing when I walked into the common room behind everyone else. When my group walked in, they talked louder, calling some over, no doubt wanting to know what happened in the lesson. I did not doubt that I would not stay a secret, no matter how much I wished it.

Shade entered the room and our gazes locked. He stood near me, but did not sit. I knew he wanted to though. He looked at me curiously once more. I did not think he could figure me out and that was fine by me.

"How come Master Diaxon is making me assist you one-on-one?" he asked finally.

I sighed. He was not even touching me and he still managed to get me turned on. "What do you mean?" I asked as I sat forward with my legs together and smoothed my dress down.

Shade looked at me curiously. "You have been here for two years, yet you have never had a lesson here and he seems to think you are too good for the others in class, plus you are twenty-one and the classes are meant only for eighteen to twenty-year-olds. I was just wondering why you are being taught instead of teaching."

I tilted my head, looking at him closely, as I chose my words carefully. How had he known I was here for two years and not taught how to fight? I opened my mouth, but he spoke first.

"I was taught here for two and a half years before I was made Master Diaxon's assistant. I saw you being escorted in."

I was sure my face paled at the words. "I did not need to be taught anything. I was home tutored at a young age, both hand-to-hand and weapon fighting and about our enemies. After I passed the trial test, Diaxon told me that you would assistant me in class because you would at least stand a chance of teaching me something rather than me teaching anyone else everything."

His eyebrows rose and he sat down, facing me. He looked at me and I knew he was looking at my piercings, no doubt wondering why I would mar my face as I had. His gaze then travelled down my body slowly.

"I guess I really shouldn't judge a book by its cover, especially yours."

I smiled, unable to help myself, and stood. "I will take that as a compliment." I walked away, out of the living accommodations and across the grass to the training building. Once inside, I pulled off my heels, placed them against the wall and then walked into the hall, my feet making no sound on the hard floor. I could fight better in bare feet. The fewer clothes I had on, the faster I could move, too.

However, I could not walk around naked. I imagine I would be the centre of attention more than I was now.

I walked straight to the weapons and took a set of four small throwing knives, ignoring the thought of what happened in the trees. I did not worry, did not feel like anything was going to go wrong and I did love knives.

I stood in front of the targets lining the wall, placed the first one into my right hand and threw it. My shot thumped directly in the middle. I did the same with my left hand. It landed close to the first one. Right or left handed, I could use both. I could hit a moving target fifty feet away and I could hit a target with two weapons from both hands.

I closed my eyes and threw two knives, one after the other. I heard the *thump, thump* as the knives hit the target. I opened my eyes. The knives were in the middle of the target, below the other two.

I walked across the room to collect the knives before I faced the targets once more, my eyes closed. The first knife left my hand, followed by the second and third at the same time. The fourth knife flew out of my hand, not for the target, but to the vampire sneaking up on me. I did not like anyone sneaking upon me.

I opened my eyes and watched him catch the knife by the end before it hit him. I raised my eyebrows, impressed. Shade had very good reflexes.

"You missed the target."

"How do you know I wasn't aiming for you?" I watched him walk toward me.

"Your change in direction before the knife left your hand."

"You were there long enough to notice that?"

"I was here when you threw the second knife. You're good with knives."

I shrugged as he held the knife out. "I always have been." I took the knife and turned away, but he grabbed my arm quickly and pulled me to him. My breath caught as a pleasant electric feeling shot down my arm and through the rest of my body, igniting a fire in the pit of my stomach and sending pleasure shooting through me.

I reacted quickly, if not badly.

I spun around under his arm and hooked my leg around his. I pulled my hand out from his grip as he fell and took a couple of steps back. Shade landed on the floor, but almost instantly flipped himself back up. He regarded me with curiosity.

I did not like to be touched as much as I disliked being sneaked up on.

"You are not with your guard."

I shrugged. "He is needed elsewhere."

"Why do you need a guard?"

I was not surprised he was asking, but tilted my head to the side as I looked at him. "You are not like other vampires." I finally said.

"How so, you don't know me."

"I do not know. You seem a lot stronger than most adult vampires, though you are my age."

"My parents are very powerful. It takes a lot to keep me down."

He walked toward me slowly, but I still backed away. I watched him walk toward the knives in the target and pull them out. He looked at me and the knife in my hand.

"Have you always been able to move quickly?" I threw the knife and it landed in the target, close to where Shade stood. He did not flinch at all.

"Always, it was the way I was brought up." He pulled that knife out and walked across the hall. Once he had the knives in their right places, he spoke again, "Have you always been able to speak Spanish?"

"I learned from Master Nikalye while he trained me, but it has gotten better in the last two years."

"And have you always not trusted people?"

"It was the way I was brought up," I quoted him.

"Why do you find it hard to trust?"

I said nothing, blood, pain, long hours of torture. I could not help but think about it. "That is personal." He walked toward me slowly, keeping his eyes locked with mine. I did not feel afraid as he neared me. I felt calm, and when he stopped close to me, I felt his breath fan across my face. I shivered a little as desire shot through me. I wanted him, that was for sure.

"Do you trust me?" he asked quietly.

I closed my eyes and took a deep breath. I could feel the heat coming off his body and the scent of his arousal. "I cannot trust you, I replied, my voice barely a whisper. His hands slipped around my waist, pulling me into his body.

"Why can't you trust me?"

"Because it is forbidden for us to lust for each other," I replied and opened my eyes so I could look at him. Years ago, there were rules made about vampires getting together. The teens could get together because they would not be able to fall pregnant. Unlike humans who had menstrual cycles before they could become pregnant, vampires did not have them until they turned twenty-one, though we grew like humans. Even then, we were different because though our bodies still released the eggs, we did not bleed. Bleeding was very dangerous for a vampire.

We were both twenty-one so risking those around us to satisfy our lust would result in punishment, despite our age—unless of course, there was a logical reason for us to be ignoring the rules.

"We can't help what our bodies want."

"What about our minds?" I asked. Our lips were very close to each other. So close, I could almost taste him.

"What does your mind want?"

He moved, pressing his lips against my own softly. Electricity shot through my entire body as I caught his bottom lip between my teeth, making him growl.

"My mind wants plenty of things, but getting in with the law is not one of them," I whispered before I smiled and walked across the hall. He followed me, walking close behind and growling a little. Once I had my shoes on, we headed outside and walked in silence, me on the grass, Shade on the path.

"Shade, where you been, man?" Lohron asked as we walked into the common room.

I passed him and headed to the feeding hall. No one I passed looked at me, and I was fine with that as I looked over my shoulder at Shade.

"Dude, I'm a tutor, we can't hang around with each other," Shade joked, making everyone laugh.

"You can't resist our good natured ways." Lohron smiled, making Shade snort out a laugh.

"The day you are good natured, Lohron, is the day I stop drinking blood."

Mmm, blood. I turned away, my stomach suddenly burning with the need to feed. I got to the feeding hall door when I felt as though someone was watching me. I looked over my shoulder and I noticed that Shade had looked over. His gaze locked with mine and I stood with my hand on the door, letting what felt like a connection wash over me. I knew Shade was feeling the same because he was not taking in a word Lohron was saying. I couldn't help but grin, flashing fangs before I looked away. I pushed open the door and walked into the hall.

The feeding hall was a large dark room full of tables and chairs. The lights were dull, lighting the place a little, but leaving many corners in shadow. At the end of the hall were shelves of food and fridges with glass doors filled with drinks, fruit and chocolates. There was also a canteen of hot food.

I walked across the hall, lost in my own thoughts. Though I had not worried about being here for the two years that I had, finally seeing the vampires had made me change my mind. I did not like being here where I could not do what I wanted, where I could not feed—and I did need to feed. I was very hungry. That was a very big problem for me because I could not get blood.

I was hungry for normal food, too. I had not eaten in two days and if I wanted to keep my strength, I had to eat, even if I could not get blood to quench my thirst. I walked past the meats and vegetables and opened one of the fridges to pick up a bowl of mixed fruit. I was hungry, but more for blood than food.

I sat in the shadows of the room in the corner and began to eat my fruit slowly, but I could not taste it. Thinking of blood had made my appetite disappear.

"Layla."

I looked up. "Hello, Diaxon." He smiled and gestured to the chair opposite me.

"May I?"

"You may."

He sat down. "You are not very hungry?" He looked at the bowl of fruit.

"I am," I replied. He nodded, knowing instantly what I was saying.

"I am sorry you have to wait to feed, we cannot just ask someone to give their blood up for you. Master Tyroz would think it was an insult, even if he does regard you highly."

I laughed. "Maybe. You came here for a reason, did you not?"

He nodded, now looking very serious. "Nikalye has spoken to me about the incident you had."

"This has something to do with why he was called out of the lesson earlier." I did not ask.

"Yes, Nikalye and I went there and when we saw what happened, he told me what happened with you."

"What has happened?"

"A young vampire, Meyahare, was found in the same location Nikalye found you when the incident with you happened," he said without falter.

"What happened to her?"

"Nothing you need to worry about."

"Diaxon," I almost growled it.

Diaxon sighed heavily. "She was found with a knife in her chest, her body was drained of blood."

My heart stopped for a second.

"What knife?"

"A black and red one."

I placed my face into my hands. Diaxon gently touched my hand.

"Nikalye will always be there with you, he will watch you even closer now. You have nothing to fear."

I stood, nearly toppling my chair over.

"I fear nothing, Diaxon. I am just tired. I like my privacy. I like my freedom."

Diaxon nodded in understanding.

"Is that all?"

"That is all." Diaxon stood.

"Goodbye," I walked around the table and headed for the door.

"Layla."

I turned.

"Be careful. It is not wise to lose control in front of the others. They do not know what you are yet."

"I will be careful." It was a promise I was not sure I could keep. I walked out of the hall and into the living area. No one in the common room noticed me as I headed toward my lift and once more, I was fine with that.

When I stepped into my lift, I felt one gaze on me, but I did not look up at Shade. I did not want to feel anything for him.

I sighed at the lie.

Chapter Seven

A loud gunshot echoed around the clearing, making me jump a little as well as making the birds in the trees fly up into the night sky. I stood still, my feet rooted firmly to the ground while my heart thumped painfully in my chest as I waited for the pain that would come. If I could stop my heart, I would. Maybe I would not need, to, maybe the shot would kill me.

No pain came.

A thud behind me made me turn around quickly, my hands instantly going to the knives on my thighs. I just touched the hilt of two when I saw a man lying on the ground with his head blown off, blood pouring out of him, his body twitching. Past him, there was a tall man half-hidden in the shadows of the trees with his gun pointed to where the man was no doubt sneaking up on me. I could not see his features, but I knew he was not happy.

"Drop all of your weapons and I will not shoot," he said, confirming what I thought.

His gun pointed at me. I swallowed and knew without a doubt that I could not dodge his bullet. Even if I could, one of the others would shoot.

Slowly, with hands calmer than myself, I bent and put my silver spear on the floor before straightening and reaching for my knives again.

"Leave those," another man said in a deep voice.

I looked at him, at his red eyes and then raised my hands in the air. The man with the gun nodded to one of his men and he stepped *forward. When he reached me, he slowly stripped me of my knives.*

"Nothing to be scared of now," he said in English with an accent.

I knew his other language was Spanish and began using it. "I'm not scared."

"Everything will be fine, Layla."

I smiled slightly, knowing we both did not agree with that.

"It is good to see you again Nikalye."

Nikalye smiled kindly and pulled me into his arms so he could hold me tight. I breathed him in, remembering the smell of him.

"I have missed you." I buried my face into his black top, holding him tight. He stroked my back gently, easing the worry inside me.

"Nikalye, Layla, come," one of the men said in English.

Nikalye looked at me with eyes that saw right through me before he smiled. He took my hand and pulled me across the clearing. I kept my head held high, trying not to look at all of the dead bodies. The dead men I had killed.

When we reached the three men, I looked at the tallest one with long black hair and red eyes.

"Father…" I said before hugging him. He did not hesitate to wrap his arms around me securely and kiss the top of my head.

"It is okay. You are safe now."

His voice rumbled when he spoke, vibrating through me. Just like Nikalye, I held him tight. I did not want to let him go and I did not want him to let me go either.

"I have missed you," I whispered. He squeezed me gently.

"And I have you." Father lifted my face so he could look at me. I knew his eyes were taking in my changed appearance. He shook his head, a sad expression on his face. "Come, let us go."

"What about this mess?" someone asked.

"I will clean up, do not worry."

I looked at Nikalye.

"You are not coming?" He stroked my face gently. I grabbed his hand, holding it tightly to my chest.

"I will not be away for long. I promise." He looked at my father.

"Take her to mine. I will look after her when you cannot."

I looked up at Father and felt a prick in my neck. I hissed and turned around, but I was too dizzy. I fell over my feet and the ground rushed at me quickly. Everything went black. I did not know if I hit the floor or not.

"I wish for her to attend lessons when she is ready, it will help take her mind off what has happened."

The voice was close but faint.

"I agree. She has been through a lot."

The voices were fading into the distance now and I felt as though I was floating in the wind. I felt as though I was the wind. Everything was black, dark, cold.

There was blood everywhere, all over my naked body. I was lying in it, soaking it up. I could still hear it dripping from the table onto the hard floor. I could not move. I could not do anything but stare blankly at the white ceiling. Saying I could not feel anything would have been a lie. I could feel the silver manacles around my wrists and ankles, holding me in place. I could feel the blood drying on my skin, making me feel sticky. I could still feel the tingle of every cut on my body, of the blood running through my veins.

Someone came into the white room. I heard the thick door open, but did not look to see who it was. I knew who it was. He leaned over me, his face blurred.

I smelled blood. I was very hungry. Fire erupted inside of me, burning me from the inside out. I struggled against my bounds, screaming.

I broke free and jumped across the room. I sank my teeth into flesh and she screamed loudly, struggling against me. Even with her strength, I was stronger. I held her tight against me while I drank her blood, quenching the thirst and the fire inside me. Her struggles grew weaker, her cries quieter. Her breathing was ragged. I heard her gurgling a little and she fell to her knees when she could not hold herself up. Her pulse was erratic, trying to pump blood through her body quickly.

I sucked on her neck hard and she moaned feebly. I continued to drink her blood, feeling her pulse slow down, feeling her life force leave her. She wasn't breathing now and there was no more blood left in her body. She was cold and I was hot.

I was still hungry.

I shoved the body away from me and stood. There were people around me. I heard their heartbeats and my mouth watered. I saw nothing but food. Food I wanted, food I planned to get.

Someone yelled and I flinched at how sad the noise sounded. A man ran forward and I backed away quickly. The heat inside, the one that hungered, was back. Pain radiated through my body, burning me once more, but I ignored it as this man knelt down in front of the girl, pulling her lifeless body into his arms. He yelled again and I knew he was mourning.

My body began to shake. I found it hard to breathe and brought my hands up to my face. I smelled blood, the blood of the girl, sweet smelling, like candyfloss. The fire in my stomach intensified. I was in unbearable agony and doubled over, holding onto my stomach. The man continued to hold the girl.

The innocent girl I killed.

With a cry that had no tears, I ran, fled, away from the males and females, away from the dead girl and away from the mourning man…

I sat up with a cry and launched myself out of bed and into Nikalye's arms. He held me close, muttering words in Spanish and comforting me until I stopped shaking. Even then, he held me still. He did not ask about what I dreamed, he would have seen it as easily as if he was actually there.

"You are not there now, *mi Belleza Oscura*." He stroked my back, easing the worry out of me until I could take a deep breath and push myself away from him, only to sink onto the bed. He followed me and placed a hand on my thigh.

I took a deep shaking breath and then stood, "I am going to shower." I needed to wash the sweat off my skin. Nikalye knew this and I knew that while I washed, he would sort out some clothes for me to wear.

I washed fully, washing the curls from my hair and shaving until I was smooth. Once I had finished, I walked back into my room. Nikalye was in the bright sunlight, sitting in my chair. I stood at my door, looking at his honey blond hair, lightened by the light of the sun while he looked outside. Distraction was all over his face. Nikalye, being a dhampir like myself, loved the sun more than anything else. He also loved a good view and I did have a good view.

I looked at my bed and saw the clothes he had placed out on it. I dried, not worried about Nikalye and then pulled on my underwear and bra before pulling on a pair of blue-white denim shorts and a grey top which hung off my shoulder. After pulling on some grey canvas shoes, I walked into my wardrobe so I could French braid my hair.

"What are we doing today?" I did not want to talk about what happened. Nikalye knew this as much as he could see the future and I knew he would not mention it. He knew I could not escape the horrors of my past.

"I need to go to my room and then I am to escort you to Diaxon."

"What's in your room?" I asked, stepping out of my wardrobe and shutting the doors.

"Nothing you have not seen. I just need a drink."

I smiled and took Nikalye's offered arm as we left my room. The lift opened instantly and it did not take long for it to get to the ground floor. When the doors opened I was blasted with laughter and cheering. I saw all the males crowded around the middle of the room and noticed that none of the females were joining in. In fact, they were not paying attention at all as they were lounging around on settees close to my lift, giggling while they painted their nails. When we walked past, they stopped and watched us. I was not surprised. Nikalye was with me after all.

We walked past the males and most of them stopped cheering to watch us, just as the females had done. I did not say anything, nor did Nikalye, though I did hear a few whispering quietly.

"Hey! Layla—"

I looked over my shoulder and saw Lohron tripping someone to the floor. The vampire—an orange eyed and messy chocolate brown haired male—grunted and rubbed the back of his head as Lohron straightened, turning around fully to look at me. I turned around to look at him. The room was quiet now and the females had gotten off their chairs and moved closer so they could watch.

"*Yes?*" I drew out the word to let him know I was in a hurry to leave.

"I figured out why you have a guard now, you're that much of a rubbish fighter that you need to be guarded so you don't get hurt."

I smiled. Though Nikalye was by my side, it amused me to hear Lohron speak about him in that way.

"If that is what you would like to think to make you feel better when I can easily knock you to the floor."

The crowd of males laughed. The smirk on Lohron's face disappeared. I did not think he expected me to speak, especially in English.

"You can't hurt me. When I get my hands on you, you'll be the one underneath me."

My smile widened.

"Saying it and doing it are two entirely different things."

Lohron looked around the room and smiled at me. "I can show you if you want me to."

"If you think you are big enough." I taunted before I turned around and walked outside, across the grass with Nikalye following me. When we got around the training building, we headed toward another one. It was large, like a mansion, close to the trees. This was where the adults stayed. Nikalye opened the door for me and I stepped inside the entrance hall—a wide square space with plush settees along the walls and paintings hanging above. Nikalye let go of the door and held his arm out for me to take.

"It is not wise to taunt the young vampires." We walked through the mansion until Nikalye opened his door and swept his hand out.

I smiled. "Thank you."

"You're welcome." Nikalye's room almost looked the same as mine, only he had no red. He had silver and gold mixed with his black. He had a bar where my walk-in wardrobe was and a black wall hid his bed from view. His window was bigger than mine, taking up two of the four sides of his room. He had no curtains. I think if he had to hide whenever the sun came out, it would make him sad.

"I did not taunt him so much." I said, replying to his earlier comment.

"Have a seat, *mi Belleza Oscura.*"

I did, sitting down on one of the seats close to the window. Nikalye walked over to his bar to collect his drink. When he sat next to me, I looked at him. "I think he will regret thinking he can fight you."

I laughed.

"I think so. too." I watched Nikalye as he drank his drink. I did not know what it was, but I knew that it was alcoholic, though it brought a question to mind. "How do you feed?" No one but Tyroz and I knew that Nikalye was a dhampir.

"Master Tyroz allows me to feed from donated blood."

"Why is it taking him so long to sort out my feeding requirements?"

"You lost control, Tyroz was there, remember?"

"How can I forget?" I looked out of the window.

Nikalye's view was very similar to mine, except the mountains were smaller on this side and not covered with snow.

"Everything will be fine," Nikalye said, touching my hand. "I will come and see you when you do not have lessons, you know that. And you can see me whenever you need, no matter what time."

"I know I can," I looked at him. "It will help me a lot if you were with me."

"I will do that. You will need me more than anything before I leave."

I frowned. "Why are you leaving?"

Nikalye smiled but only slightly. "Some of the royals are coming to visit—"

My jaw dropped. "Why?"

"*Mi Belleza Oscura*—"

"Nikalye," I growled.

"Some of us are going out. We need guards to watch over you and the Lords and Ladies are providing us with that."

I turned to look at him in shock. "Going where?"

"You know where," he said it gently, but that did not stop the fear from setting in deep in my soul.

"Do not go, Nikalye."

"I have to, I have to." He told me in both English and Spanish, telling me how serious that actually was.

"But what if you do not come back?" Nikalye took my hand in both of his and turned me around so I was looking directly at him. I looked into his eyes and watched as the red ring around the white-blue flashed before returning to normal.

"I cannot be taken down easily, you should know this."

I nodded, still feeling the fear inside. Fear that Nikalye would not come back to me alive, despite what he saw in his vision.

"When will Father visit?" I asked.

"When the time is right, *mi Belleza Oscura.*"

"I miss him." Nikalye pulled me to him and kissed the top of my head. He did not say anything because he did not need to. We stayed in silence before I could not take it any longer.

With a sigh, I stood. "I am glad I can come to you when I need to."

"As am I." He stood and once again offered his arm.

I took it and we headed out of the room.

Chapter Eight

$\mathcal{I}$ thought of Father as we walked out of the building. I missed him dearly. I wished he could be here with me, would feel better with him protecting me, but could not make it known about who I was. I would be in danger if I did so.

I did not have to worry about being in danger from Mother. She was dead, just as Nikalye said she was when I thought she was the one who tried to stab me. She could no longer torment me or try to kill me. If it were not for Mother, I would not be here, surrounded with no way of getting out—not with the guards posted around the perimeter of this place.

During the day and night, there were creatures known as Shadow Demons. They were not human in any form or way, though they could take the form of a human if they needed to speak. They were entirely invisible to all eyes unless they wished themselves visible and when they were, they are exactly what their names said—a shadow. Their own kind could see one another.

Even if you could sense the Shadow Demons, there was no way to get past them. They did not fail when they had a task to do. Anyone foolish enough to attempt such a thing faced the Shadow Demons.

It was a horrible way to die.

"I think you are late once again to your lesson," Nikalye

mused as we looked around the empty common room. I laughed a little as we turned and headed back out of the building and into the training one.

"Ah, Miss Layla, good of you to join us," Diaxon said.

I smiled at him and walked across the room to where Shade was standing, avoiding his eyes. Nikalye stood close behind me.

"Okay, now I would like to show Layla how this lesson works so I want you to get into two groups. The leaders will pick someone from their group, or themselves, and then they will fight. You can choose anyone you wish, but be warned, Nikalye, Shade and I will be taking points."

"So this is just like a practical fighting game?" Kalitha asked.

"If you wish to see it that way, yes," Diaxon said. "Layla, if you will stand out so you can see what is being done."

I nodded.

"Kalitha, Gutax, select who you would like in your group." He pointed to them both and then backed up to lean against the wall.

Nikalye rubbed my arms before walking over to him, leaving me and Shade watching the others closely. Kalitha pointed to Lohron. His friends clapped him on the back as he passed. He reached the female as Gutax picked.

"Kiuthil."

I was surprised he had chosen her, but the reason became apparent when she kissed him. Everyone hooted and Diaxon cleared his throat loudly. They broke apart, but they were not embarrassed. Vampires were not easily embarrassed with things like that.

"Would you choose another," Shade said to Lohron with amusement.

"Niaxoz," he said instantly.

I walked over to the wall and leaned against it while

everyone got into his or her group.

Once everyone was, Shade spoke again. "Leaders, decide who you will choose first. Once that is decided, they will choose someone from their own team and that person will choose someone from the opposite team. Whoever wins, chooses someone from the opposite team, and so on."

Both leaders spoke in low voices for a couple of seconds before deciding to flip a coin. Lohron's team chose tails. They won. Kalitha picked Berlox. He chose to fight Leidon. Berlox was a lot bigger and no doubt stronger than Leidon, but I was betting Leidon was a lot quicker, just as he told me. I thought the other team would win.

Everyone backed off, leaving the two in the middle of the hall. They shook hands before circling each other. Berlox made the first move, launching his large body at Leidon, who dodged it easily, leaving Berlox to run straight past him. Berlox turned and threw his fist toward Leidon's face. He ducked and threw his own fist forward. He hit Berlox in the stomach and then quickly hooked his leg around Berlox's large one, tripping him up before pinning his hands above his head with his feet.

Leidon's team cheered loudly.

"Leidon, choose a member from the opposite team."

Leidon walked over to his team and had a quiet discussion before looking at the opposite team. "Zhanju."

The red haired vampire stepped forward. They both shook hands before stepping back and circling each other. Zhanju spun around, kicking his feet out like a martial artist. Leidon ducked when Zhanju kicked high and then he swept his feet out, knocking his feet from underneath him. Zhanju hit the floor, but flipped himself back up fast and punched Leidon, who just grabbed his fist, twisted it around and then tripped him up. He pinned his hands to the floor and their team cheered.

Leidon stood and pointed to Teigan. They both walked into the middle of the hall and bumped fists. Teigan attacked instantly and had Leidon on the floor in less than a second. The cheer from their team was deafening. Leidon shook his head.

"I should have seen that coming," Leidon said, making Teigan laugh.

"You'll remember next time."

"Choose someone from the opposite team," Shade said.

He did so, choosing the handsome Niaxoz. I watched as they both moved around each other before attacking. Teigan was quick, but so was Niaxoz. It took Teigan ten minutes to pin Niaxoz to the floor. He chose another one and again, did not have to do much, but use his speed to pin him. I think the others were nervous about fighting Teigan it seemed.

It was a pity I was not fighting him. I think I would have enjoyed myself. I walked across the room and stood near Nikalye and Diaxon. They both glanced at me, but only Diaxon looked away.

"*Mi, Belleza Oscura*. What can I do for you?"

"I'm bored," I said truthfully.

Nikalye chuckled and shook his head. "You were never one to stay out of a fight."

"That is true," I agreed.

"I will make sure you have someone to fight during your next practical lesson." Nikalye watched Teigan pin someone to the floor quickly. His team cheered loudly and he bowed with a smile on his face.

"You are not worried?" I asked, he looked at me and searched my face.

"I will always worry, *mi Belleza Oscura*, but I have to let you live. If I do not, it will make things worse."

"But won't fighting make it worse?"

"You do not want to fight?"

"No I do. You know that, but I won't put everyone in danger by doing so."

Nikalye nodded slowly. "I understand. No, it will not make it worse. Fighting will get a lot of stuff off your chest, stuff that I should have helped release when I first brought you here. It will only get bad if blood is drawn. You are not feeding for reasons you know. If you should start, you will not stop."

I looked over at the others as Teigan's team cheered when the remaining female, Arezon, was carefully pinned to the mat. Teigan helped her to her feet before he pointed to Lohron, the remaining male on the team left to fight. They both circled each other before Teigan attacked. Lohron moved quickly, dodging his attack and kicked out. Teigan blocked his attack, but did not block Lohron's next attack. He fell to the floor and just as quickly as it started, Lohron had him pinned. His team cheered as he helped Teigan to his feet. They bumped fists before Lohron chose someone from the opposite team, Gutax. It did not take him long to pin him to the mat, nor did it take him long to pin any of the others. It seemed Lohron was indeed a good fighter.

"Well done," Diaxon said. "I think next time I'll mix the lesson up a little so everyone can have a demonstration of how well Miss Layla here fights."

I looked around and saw Lohron looking at me with a smirk.

"This lesson is finished. Either Myself or Shade will be coming to escort you back here later." Diaxon walked across the room, opened the door and waited for everyone to leave. They all talked and laughed about what happened on the way back. I stayed behind and Nikalye stayed with me. Diaxon nodded to both of us before shutting the door behind him.

"Come, let us fight," Nikalye said while he pulled off his

leather jacket.

I smiled and walked into the middle of the hall. I stretched up, going onto the tips of my toes before I bent forward, touching them.

Nikalye walked up to me and bowed at the waist before setting his feet apart and putting his fists in the air.

I smiled and did the same. I touched my left wrist with his right and then grabbed him quickly. He was expecting a quick move, but he was not expecting me to use the simplest way of getting him to the floor.

"You should always expect everything, Master Nikalye." I backed away from him after knocking him to the floor. He laughed and I knew I was right in thinking that he had not expected the move.

He got to his feet. "*Mi Belleza Oscura*, pin for a point."

I smiled and tilted my head to the side while he walked toward me. I sprang and he grunted when I knocked him to the floor and pinned his hands there. Nikalye burst out laughing, making me smile.

"You should have been ready. You don't know when your enemy is going to attack."

"Point," he laughed and then pushed me off with enough force to launch me across the room.

I twisted in midair and landed lightly on my feet as he ran at me with his vampire speed. I twisted around and kicked out hard, hitting Nikalye in the stomach and knocking him into the wall so hard, he bounced away from it. I put my arm around his neck and jumped, swinging around him and knocking him to the floor. Nikalye moved fast and reversed our positions so he was on top and I was on the bottom. He pinned me.

"Point," I said, smiling. Nikalye smiled back and got off, pulling me to my feet. We walked back into the middle of the hall once more. Nikalye punched and I ducked before jumping into the air and swinging my foot out. I hit him in the side of his head and then knocked him to the floor when I swept his feet out from underneath him. I took a couple of steps back while Nikalye got to his feet.

I blew him a kiss and he smiled with fangs and then ran at me. I twisted away, but he twisted with me. I punched and he ducked before jumping out of range of my kick. He ducked again when I twisted around, kicking my leg in a circle and then grabbed me from behind, pinning my arms behind my back. I head butted him, but he moved his head, having already anticipated the move.

"Cheater."

"Use whatever skill you have, *mi Belleza Oscura*. That was the first thing your father and I taught you." He let go and backed away.

I turned slowly, watching him. He smiled before motioning me forward. I walked slowly, trying to block my thoughts from him. He moved as I moved and grabbed my leg before slamming me into the floor.

"Cheater," I repeated.

"Learn to block your thoughts, *mi Belleza Oscura*. You are a great fighter, use what you have."

He pulled me to my feet before backing away. I took a deep breath and blew out slowly. I motioned for Nikalye to come as I set my feet apart. I kept my eyes on him as he moved and when he was near, I punched. He grabbed my arm and flipped me over him. I hit the floor hard, but pushed him around and pinned him before he could pin me.

"Point," I said.

"Well done. I did not see that coming."

"I learned from the best."

"Indeed."

I climbed off and we faced each other once more.

"You should teach everyone this."

"They are already being taught how to fight."

"I meant fighting you when you know what their moves are going to be. It will make them stronger, even if they are not going to be fighting you."

"This is true."

"I am never wrong, Nikalye."

"I will consider this and speak with Diaxon."

I smiled and then launched myself at him. He grabbed me and slammed me into the floor, hard. I groaned as he pinned me.

"How did you know?"

Nikalye laughed. "Talking does not distract me from what your mind is saying."

I kicked Nikalye as he stepped away from me and he fell to the floor. I jumped on him quickly and pinned him.

"Point," I said just as the door to the hall opened and Diaxon walked in, followed by a group of vampires. He raised his eyebrows when he saw us, but otherwise did not say a word. The teens whispered to each other and cast curious glances our way as I got off Nikalye. He walked across the hall with me following. As he grabbed his jacket, he had a quiet word with Diaxon before we both walked out of the hall.

"I am going to have a meeting with Diaxon later on. I will mention what you said to him."

I smiled. Nikalye held open the door to the living accommodations and I walked past. Everyone in the room became silent, watching us as we crossed the room. I glanced at Shade and he smiled at me slightly before I looked away. When I got to my lift, I put my pin in and turned to Nikalye. "Are you coming or going?"

Nikalye took my hand and placed a kiss on it. "I must take my leave. I will see you in your next lesson."

I nodded and smiled. I could hear the whispers around

me. "Goodbye, Nikalye."

"*Adios, mi Belleza Oscura*," He smiled before he walked away.

I stepped into my lift and pressed the button. My eyes found Shade's before the lift doors shut. I hoped I would get to fight him, to see how well he could truly fight.

Chapter Nine

I headed out of my room early. I was early because Nikalye was not waiting for me in or outside my room, nor was he in the common room when my lift doors swept open. The common room was still as full as what it was when I went into my room. I walked through the room past everyone, ignoring the stares and whispers. When I got outside, I knew some of them were looking out of the window, watching me walking across the grass.

I walked around the training building when I heard someone walking behind me. I turned and saw that it was Shade. I knew he had not followed me to attack me, so I stopped and leaned against the wall so he could catch up. He stood in front of me and I saw him gaze as he always did when he saw me.

"Why did you follow me?"

He shrugged. "Curious. Why are you shadowed by Master Nikalye?"

"You have already asked me this."

He shrugged again. "Curious."

I looked into his silver eyes, drawn in before I could look away. "He does what he wishes." I decided to tell him the partial truth.

"He must be following you for a reason."

"His reasons are his own."

Shade looked to his right, toward the building Nikalye's

room was in. "You go to him even when he is not with you."

I looked to my left at the building and sighed. Yes, I was going to see Nikalye before going to my lesson. "He is the only one I know here, Shade."

"But that's not the reason you seek him out."

I looked back at him with a little amazement. "What makes you think that?"

Shade shrugged and smiled slightly, revealing the points of his fangs. "You're easy to read."

"You're lying." I narrowed my gaze slightly.

He chuckled a little.

I looked back at the building before walking away from it and through the trees. I stopped when I got to the spot I found the knife and where the vampire — Meyahare — was found a couple of hours later, killed by the same knife. I could smell her blood. It was faint but here.

"Some of the others are talking about you," Shade said after a while.

I turned to look at him. He was leaned against one of the trees, his arms crossed over his muscular chest, looking at me.

"Me? Why?"

Shade smiled. He obviously liked the fact that he had my attention. "They saw you and Master Nikalye in the hall."

"Ah yes, them." I nodded, remembering when the others walked in while Nikalye and I were fighting.

"They think you are both involved."

I laughed, I could not help it. The thought of Nikalye and me being together was a funny thought. He liked a good-looking female when he saw one, and he did see me as one, but he would never see me in that way.

"For starters, I am twenty-one. I can be with who I choose to be with, despite the rules." He raised his eyebrows. "We were fighting and I pinned him when they walked in."

"You and Master Nikalye were fighting?" Shade asked, his eyebrows rising higher into his hair.

"Yes," I nodded. "Because I did not get to fight during the lesson so Nikalye let me fight him." I shrugged. I fought Nikalye all the time, it was not a big deal—not to me anyway.

"And you pinned him?"

"Yes."

"Master Nikalye?"

"Yes." I ignored the disbelief in his tone.

"I take it you like to fight."

I smiled. "I love to fight."

"You do not mind whether you fight hand-to-hand or with weapons?"

"I do not, no. Fighting is fighting."

"We are more alike than I thought."

I smiled widely. He stepped close to me and put his hands either side of my head, leaning against the trunk of the tree behind me.

"And I do not believe you and Master Nikalye are involved."

It was my turn to raise my eyebrows. "And you say this because?" He pressed himself against me, pressing me against the tree, and put his lips close to mine. I closed my eyes and parted my lips as my breath became heavier and my body heated with pleasure.

"If you were with Master Nikalye, you would not be reacting to me as you are."

Pleasure shot through my entire body at his words and my stomach squirmed with longing. The need to touch his skin was strong, which was something I had never felt before, but Shade was right, I could not help what my body wanted.

"You are impossibly handsome. I am sure all the females

fall to their knees at the sight of you."

"I've had no female fall to my feet if I don't wish them to. You are the first in a long time who I wish to fall to her knees."

I opened my eyes to look at him. "And what would you achieve, getting me to my knees?"

He grinned, flashing his fangs and kissed me hard, making the pleasure slowly travel around my body and intensify.

"If you are on your knees, I will have a good view of you taking me into your mouth with those luscious lips of yours," he said against my lips.

I moaned and ran my hands through his hair before kissing him. He slipped one of his hands around the back of my neck and put the other one on my back, pushing me into him. He pressed himself into me and I gasped at the sensation of how he felt. He slipped his tongue past my lips and entwined it with mine. I tasted him, felt him and I wanted more.

"We cannot do this," I said, breaking the kiss despite my feelings. His lips went to my neck, even as he grunted his reply.

"No one is with us. We will only get into trouble if we are caught."

I tilted my head to give him better access even as my hands went to the zip of his jeans. I undid it as pleasure shot through me, and felt his erection twitch before I grabbed it, running my fingers from base to tip, feeling the stiffness, and smoothness. I smiled when he groaned and pushed himself into my hand.

"We can't do this," I whispered, smoothing my thumb across the pearl of liquid at the head, rubbing it into his skin and making him growl.

"And yet you are not stopping." He looked at me then,

heat swirling in the silver of his eyes.

I grinned and leaned forward to bite his lip before I dropped to my knees and took him into my mouth. His groan echoed around the trees as I took him deep and sucked on him hard. His hands went to my hair, bunching it up into and pushing me into him. I let him, taking him in deeper this time before he pulled on my hair. I felt my body heating up and growing wet at the taste of him. Pleasure travelled through my entire body, making me want more of him.

I licked him from base to tip and sucked on the spot where his pulse beat erratically. Shade groaned, his hands leaving my hair so he could brace them on the tree trunk. I took him into my mouth again, letting my lips and tongue slide slowly down the length of him.

"You're going to have to stop," Shade said in a breathless voice as he tried to speak in a normal tone. "I don't think I'm going to last much longer."

At his words, I took him faster and sucked harder, making him groan once more. I felt him pulse, harden more in my mouth, and when I scraped my fangs along the length of him, making his pulse jump beneath my fangs, he gripped my hair tightly as he came. I continued to suck on him, swallowing his semen until there was none left. He groaned when I slid him out of my mouth, still sucking, taking the last drops of come. I licked my lips as I stood and Shade pulled me close to him.

"You're bad."

"We are also late. You have a lesson to teach. Everyone is most probably already there." That brought a smile to his face before I walked away. He did not follow straight away and I was sure that was because he was sorting himself out.

Diaxon stopped speaking to Nikalye as I walked in. I was surprised to see Nikalye in the hall instead of looking for me. Both of them looked my way and I nodded to Diaxon before nodding to Nikalye. After glancing at Shade when he walked into the room, he nodded back.

"Right, as I have told the others," Diaxon said to Shade and I, "there is a change of plan with this lesson. We will be doing another hand-to-hand combat session. This is because someone was thrown into the weapons and they were taken out of the hall, as you can see." He gestured over to the wall where it was bare. "But Master Nikalye and I have been speaking and we decided that you can both join in. This is because you," he looked at me, "have already seen how this game works. And if you fight also," he said to Shade. "This will show us how much everyone else has learned."

I threw Nikalye a big smile and he smiled back.

"Shade, go to that group," Diaxon gestured over to the group with Leidon and Lohron in. "Layla, that one if you please."

I walked over to stand near the opposite group. I was still wearing my baggy grey top so I pulled it over to the side, the opposite side to where it hung off my shoulder, and tied it into a knot.

"Leidon choose someone from the opposite team to fight," Diaxon called as he and Nikalye retreated to the end of the hall.

I saw Shade lean in and everyone else followed as he whispered. Lohron glanced at me when both Shade and Leidon nodded before Leidon walked into the middle of the hall.

"Layla…"

Chapter Ten

I walked forward and smiled at Lohron, my decision already made.

"You're next."

"What makes you confident you'll win?"

I kept my smile in place, but did not answer. I looked at Leidon and nodded. He nodded back before circling me. I stayed still as stone as he did so. When he made his move, I simply stepped to the side, twisting my body at the same time, and grabbed his arm. I stuck my foot in front of his and he fell onto his side, hard. Still holding his arm, I leaned over him without bending my legs and pinned his arms above his head.

"Now *that* I didn't see coming," he said, seeming to be sincerely impressed.

I laughed and let him go. I straightened and he gave me a curious look before getting to his feet. I looked at Lohron as he walked away and raised my pierced eyebrow. His team cheered him on as he walked forward. He gave me a smug look.

"I'll try to go easy," I told him.

He snorted. "Like I said, I'll prove it. Your guard isn't allowed to step in and help."

"I don't need a guard when I know you cannot touch me."

Lohron gave a smug look. "I'll be a gentleman and let you

have the first hit."

"I am sure that is a very hard thing for you to do. Be a gentleman that is." I heard sniggers across the room.

Lohron glared before walking forward. He moved behind me and lifted his foot to knock the backs of my legs, but before he could even touch me, I twisted to the side and hooked mine around his. I pushed hard onto his chest and slammed him into the floor. I stepped back and watched him get to his feet. The room was silent now, shocked at what they had just seen.

"As I said, you cannot touch me."

This made Lohron angry. He moved forward fast and threw his fist toward my head. I moved my head to the side and grabbed his wrist. I twisted myself under his arm and twisted his arm behind his back and pushed him hard, making him stagger forward. He turned slowly and regarded me with interest, if a little angry.

"You're faster than you look."

"And I am bored." I ran at him and slammed him into the floor before he even realised I had moved. His hands were pinned underneath my own not even a second later. I climbed off him and looked at Nikalye.

"Layla."

"Only interfere if there is blood," I told him in Spanish so the others did not understand.

He glanced at Shade before nodding.

"Agreed."

I turned and pointed to Shade.

He grinned and stepped forward. "What makes you think I'll be any good?"

I let my eyes travel down his body slowly, remembering the hardness of him in my mouth and the rising pleasure shooting through me at his touch.

"Oh I think you'll be amazing," I said, looking into his

eyes. He smiled slightly, heat swirling in the silver once more. He was remembering what happened also.

"You have not seen me fight."

"You cannot be much worse than this lot," I replied.

"Much? I can easily put you on the floor."

I grinned. "It is much harder to put me on the floor."

"I could remind you that I have seen you on your knees."

The room whistled and hooted at his words, but I knew they were not catching onto the fact that something had happened between us.

"And I could remind you that I was in control, where as you were not." I licked my lips.

He grinned and stepped forward. "We'll see who is in control by the end."

"Yes, we will."

He ran at me, kicking out. I ducked and then lifted my leg up high behind me, the back of my foot hit the back of his head as my hand touched the ground. I pushed myself up fast, twisted around and caught his outstretched arm. I then hooked my leg around his, causing him to fall forward. I took a step back.

"Don't go easy on me please," I said as he flipped himself back onto his feet. The whole room was even quieter now, everyone was looking at me in shock. I did not think anyone had seen Shade hit before.

Shade smiled slightly and circled me. I stayed still and tracked him, but he moved faster than what I thought he could. I found my cheek pressed against the wall and my arm twisted behind my back. Shade's body was against me and his hot breath was near my ear.

"Do not worry, I don't plan on going easy on you."

He pushed himself against me, making me hiss. Whether it was with annoyance or pleasure as the electricity I felt with his touch shot through my hands and down my arms, I did not know. Maybe it was both.

"I bet you like it rough."

Shade's whisper caused me to shiver. An ache had begun to form in between my legs, where I very much wanted him to touch me.

He chuckled and backed off.

I turned slowly and watched him move into the middle of the hall. I circled him before jumping into the air and kicking out. He ducked and then blocked my punch. I jumped back, dodging his kick, then kicked out three times, one after the other. Shade blocked my moves again and as I landed, I dropped to the floor and swept his legs out from underneath him.

I backed away and circled him as he flipped to his feet again. He punched and I moved out of reach before sending one of my own, which he dodged easily. He twisted around, lifting his leg up and I bent backward, dodging his foot, until my hands touched the floor. I pushed myself up fast and kicked him, but he was fast to react and moved out of range before kicking out again. I back flipped before jumping and twisting. My kick landed in his face and he staggered back. I jumped forward and tripped him up. As he fell, I jumped on him, but he lifted his legs at the last second and I flew over his body.

The vampires standing around scattered quickly as I flew across the room. I hit the floor hard. Both my right shoulder and hip took the blow before I rolled onto my feet. I knew straight away my hip was going to bruise, but it did not hurt when I put weight on it. My arm did not have such luck. I had dislocated it and it was hurting.

Shade got to his feet, but did not move. He knew he had hurt me and I knew he thought we should stop.

Nikalye stepped forward, but I glared. He stopped moving and looked at me for a second before retreating to his corner. He agreed that he would only interfere if there were blood. There was not.

I grabbed my arm, but knew, even as strong as I was, I would not be able to put my arm back into the socket right. I looked at the wall next to me.

"Don't," Shade warned, obviously aware of what I was going to do.

I ignored him and launched myself at the wall. Shade ran forward, but I got to the wall first. My shoulder slammed into it hard and my arm popped painfully. In anger, I punched Shade hard in the face when he reached me. My fist landed in his face so powerfully, his feet left the ground. I fell to my knees. The pain was immense, my arm was tingling and my fingers had gone numb.

I got to my feet the same time Shade did. I looked at him as I moved my arm in a circular motion. I didn't wince with pain even though my arm hurt. When I next hit him, it was stronger and faster. He likewise moved faster and dodged each of my blows—we were evenly matched in hand-to-hand combat. where I lacked in weight, I made up for with my speed, just as Leidon had done. I was able to knock him to the floor a couple more times, but could not pin him. He managed to knock me into the wall, but he, too, could not pin me.

He kicked out and I spun around, but was not fast enough. His kick landed on my injured hip the same time my kick landed in his stomach hard. He staggered backward and I dropped to my knees once more. Shade ran at me so fast, I could not see him. Then suddenly, I was airborne, flying backward while my shoulder flared with pain. I smashed into the wall with enough force to knock me forward, but Shade was there in a second, slamming me into the wall again. He lifted my arms above my head and my shoulder screamed with pain, but I did not show that I was hurting. Instead, I growled deep in my throat. The sound vibrated down to my chest, making my heartbeat faster. I kicked out because he did not have hold of my legs, but he dodged the blow. I growled again.

"I hope you know that when I get close enough, I'm going to make you bleed."

Shade smiled.

I lifted my leg up high and his head snapped back. His hands loosened around my wrists. I quickly spun around and kicked him in the stomach. He fell down, but not for long. In a second, he was on me and in another, he was slamming me into the wall again, harder this time.

"You are not going to get a chance," Shade told me.

"I'll suck you dry!" I was angry, I didn't even know what I was saying. I had never before been pinned so many times by someone my age. It was rather annoying. I saw Shade's eyebrows rise in surprise before he spun me around in his grip. He pushed himself against me and my cheek was against the wall again. My arms were pinned above my head.

"Oh yeah, but I thought you wanted my blood," Shade said, joking.

He did not say it as loudly as what I had, but I knew that the others could not hear what we were saying. I pushed myself back against him and found myself reacting to the feel of him. This just angered me further. I pushed myself against him hard enough to push him back.

He was strong, but I was smarter. As he pushed me forward, I ran up the wall and flipped backward over his head. I slammed him into the floor and rolled backward onto my feet. He flipped himself up and turned to face me. I ran at him, but he twisted and slammed me into the wall again.

"I bet you like getting people up against the wall," I said, struggling against his hold.

"I have never had anyone up against the wall," Shade said seriously and then glanced down at our touching bodies and smiled. "Except you, if you behave, I will do more than pin you."

I laughed before head butting him. He kicked out as I ran away from him and I tripped. Shade grabbed my ankles as I fell to the floor and he pulled me back while I hissed at him. He grabbed my hips and held me against his body. I sighed. I could feel him pressed against me, feel the blood pumping through his veins. I realised that he, like me, was running out of breath, making his pulse beat fast.

I noted all of this and it made me hungry.

I couldn't stop myself from putting my head against the cold floor and I couldn't help the sigh that came out of my mouth or the curling of my fists when Shade moved against me. He noticed this because he moved against me again. My body reacted and I was instantly aroused.

"Oh, you like this, do you?"

His pelvis moved in a circular motion against me. My skin broke out in goose bumps. My breath caught and I hissed with frustration.

I heard Shade lick his lips and his hands gripped me in a different way, not to hold me, but to move me. Flipping me over before I could react and get away from him, Shade gripped my hips tight as I automatically wrapped my legs around his waist. He pulled me further into him, but before I could flip him over and pin his hands above his head, he rubbed himself against me, making pleasure shoot through my entire body. A surprised gasp escaped my lips.

Shade's eyes opened a little with surprise.

"Don't—" I breathed.

Shade leaned over me, rubbing against me further and pinned my arms above my head. I hissed and tried to bite him as the others cheered and clapped because I had lost this fight.

"Well done, Shade. Okay, I think that will be all for tonight. Single file, head to the feeding hall." Diaxon and Nikalye herded everyone out of the room.

When the door shut, Shade and I were alone. Shade grabbed my attention when he pushed himself against me again, making me gasp and shut my eyes.

Shade reacted and his body hardened. "Why?" he whispered, obviously wondering about my earlier outburst. His voice was low, almost a growl.

I shuddered, my skin heating up, and became instantly wet as pleasure travelled through my body, ending in between my legs with a little pulse. I swallowed and opened my eyes.

He was smiling.

"I need to feed," I said because it was the only thing I could think to say to get him off me. He looked at me curiously, not loosening his grip. I saw him run his tongue almost teasingly along the points of his fangs and I smelled the blood a second later.

My lips parted and my eyes widened.

His eyebrows rose and he tilted his head to the side. "That is why you are different. You are a dhampir."

"Yes," I panted the word. His wound had already healed, but I could still smell the aroma of his blood. To others, vampire and human, they would smell copper. To me, the smell was sweet, the smell of man and life.

I expected him to let go of me. He surprised me, looking at me curiously before he leaned down and put his lips close to mine. Not only could I still smell his blood, I could also smell him and I wanted both. I found my lips parting, ready for him to close the distance between us. Shade waited before putting his lips against mine. The kiss was slow, sweet, but demanding at the same time. He slipped his tongue into my mouth as he kissed me and ran it along my fang. When the blood hit my tongue, it sent a burst of flavour—and pleasure—shooting through me. I closed my eyes and moaned while I sucked on his tongue hard. I was only a little aware that Shade's arousal was climbing higher and higher. That turned me on more.

I sucked harder and he pushed himself into me. I moaned into his mouth and my back arched off the floor. Shade's grip on my hands tightened. I gave another big pull and Shade took a deep breath before slowly sliding his tongue out of my mouth. He moved away, but I moved quickly, catching him by surprise. I pushed him into the floor and held him there. He grabbed my hands, pushing up so he could sit up. He pinned them behind my back, making my chest stick out dangerously close to his face.

"Little Dhampir." He moved both of my hands in one of his, grabbed the back of my neck with his free hand and pulled me to him. He kissed me hard, I could still taste the blood on his tongue. When pleasure shot through me, I moaned into his mouth. He pulled my body further into him before he moved away.

I growled. I wanted more. I eyed his neck, but he shook his head.

"I know you have not been fed, and I would feed you, but you know what will happen." He was correct. If anyone was to find out Shade fed me his blood, Tyroz would speak to me personally and do something worse than Shade could possibly imagine. He would expose who I was.

I said nothing. I looked at Shade's handsome features as he ran his finger over my cheek, making me close my eyes against the pleasure rising inside. Shade leaned forward to kiss me when we heard voices from the other side of the door. With a curse, he pushed himself to his feet, me still wrapped around him. He lowered me to the floor and kept hold of my hands as I tested my weight on my leg. Shade's blood, a tiny portion that it was, had taken the pain away from my shoulder and hip.

The door opened and another group walked into the hall. All of them greeted Shade with respect as I walked away. He did not stop to chat, but followed me out of the hall.

When we walked into the empty common room, I headed straight for my lift. I intended to have a long hot shower and then sleep so I could recover my energy quicker. Without blood, it would take me longer. I would be fine within a couple of hours.

"Little Dhampir."

I turned and look at Shade standing by the double doors of the feeding hall.

"You are not going to eat?"

"I have no appetite for food."

"You must eat something, for your energy."

I shook my head and pressed the lift button. "I only wish for one thing and I cannot have it." I looked at Shade's neck. Remembering how his blood tasted and how it made me react was arousing once more. I remembered his kiss, his soft lips against my own. I wanted that kiss everywhere.

"I enjoyed fighting someone who could actually hit me," I said honestly.

He smiled. "I enjoyed that feeling, too."

We looked at each other. His words stirred something deep inside me. Something that made me shiver with pleasure. I turned away and walked into the lift without another word. I leaned against the wall as soon as the doors shut.

I was in trouble. I needed Shade's touch. No, I wanted Shade's touch and, like the blood, I could not have it.

Chapter Eleven

"Y̶ou are not happy, *mi Belleza Oscura*. What is wrong?" Nikalye said from my door. I opened my eyes to look at him, not shocked to see him at all. I was, after all, meant to be in a lesson.

"No I am not," I admitted. "A lot of things have been on my mind lately."

"Quite understandable," Nikalye said as he came toward me. I moved across my bed so he could lie down next to me and draw me in his arms. "It has been a long time, too long, since I saw you happy as you were."

I looked up at him. "I am happy now, am I not?"

"You have not been happy in a long time, *mi Belleza Oscura*."

"But I am happy with you, and with Father."

Nikalye smiled. "That is true." He stroked my cheek. "So why are you not happy now?"

I did not answer.

Nikalye knew what was wrong. He chose not to say anything, but just to hold me in his arms, comforting me as he had always done, even when I did not need it. He was always there and knew how to make a situation better in the end.

Nikalye got of the bed and crossed my room. I sat up, frowning. Obviously, Nikalye had sensed something I had not. He opened the door and I saw Diaxon standing outside my door, his fist raised.

"Master Nikalye," Diaxon bowed. "Layla," he bowed again.

"Come in, Diaxon," I said, sitting up and crossing my legs.

Diaxon bowed his head and stepped into my room. Nikalye remained standing now, posing as a guard rather than a friend.

"Layla, people are wondering where you are."

"Shade is wondering where you are, *mi Belleza Oscura*," Nikalye said, a knowing glint in his eyes.

I smiled before speaking to Diaxon. "I am incredibly hungry. I did not think it wise to join a group of fighting vampires with the risk of exposing what I really am."

Diaxon bowed his head. "Understandable, I shall inform Shade that you are tired so he does not suspect. The boy is very wise."

"He knows," I said. Nikalye looked at me sharply, but said nothing.

"Are you sure that's wise?"

"He cut himself while we were fighting, he saw how I reacted. I am incredibly hungry, as I've said." I did not say it kindly. Talking about blood was making my stomach burn with fire and my gums throb.

"Perhaps you should go and inform those who are left wondering and I shall speak to Layla," Nikalye said, bowing his head a little.

"Of course," he turned his attention onto me. "Will you be joining us tomorrow?"

"I think I should be fine. Some sleep will help," I said, smiling a little to reassure him.

"Very well, Layla," he bowed his head and turned to Nikalye. "Master Nikalye." They bowed to each other and then Diaxon left, closing the door behind him. Nikalye looked at me and placed his finger over his lip. I waited, keeping my eyes on Nikalye until he removed his finger.

"Why did you not tell me about the boy knowing?"

I raised my pierced eyebrow. "You were out of the room when it happened and I have not seen you until now. Besides, I thought you knew."

"I knew of…some things, *mi Belleza Oscura*, but this, I did not know."

"What do you mean?"

"Your mind has been elsewhere, on the boy, on trust."

"Can I trust him?" I asked the question instantly because fear was setting deep within, like ice.

"The boy's mind is hard to read, much like your own, though for different reasons."

"So you do not know?"

"Nothing in the future is sure, *mi Belleza Oscura*."

"Which means?"

Nikalye looked at me for a while before speaking. "Trust your own instincts when you cannot trust anything else, or when you are not entirely sure."

"My instincts have never been wrong." I agreed with a nod.

"And they never will be." Nikalye smiled. He crossed the room and sat on the edge of my bed. "Why were you thinking about that time?"

I shrugged. Before Nikalye arrived, I had been thinking about Father, and Mother training me together. It was the only time they had been together during one of my training session and they had given an example of how compatible they were in battle. It was amazing to watch.

I knew that Nikalye would know whether I was lying or not so I answered him truthfully. "When I fought Shade, I was frustrated and mad. I am not used to fighting someone like an equal. After you all left and he cut himself, I was instantly hungry, as I always am when it comes to blood. I was thinking about that time because I was trying to remember what it felt like not to get hungry so easily, not even when I was badly injured."

"And can you remember?" he asked softly. He knew this was a touchy subject for me.

"Yes and no. It was a long time ago, before the bad started happening. A lot happened and instead of being able to forget about the pain and remember my life before, it is the opposite. I am forgetting bits of my past, but cannot forget about the pain." I shook my head wearily. I had not told Nikalye anything about my worries, but he knew. He was always telling me stories so I could not forget, and for that, I was grateful. Without the memories, I knew I would never have a chance of truly healing.

"I will always be here to chase away those nightmares, *mi Belleza Oscura*. Nothing can harm you where it truly hurts." Nikalye took my hands and stroked them with his thumb.

"But it is the nightmares of my past that truly hurt, Nikalye. It is the nightmares I long to run away from, to forget."

"And you will, when the day comes for revenge."

I grinned widely. "That day cannot come any sooner."

Nikalye chuckled softly and pulled me off the bed. "That day will be the day everyone fears you, not for what you are, but because they will be able to smell the anger coming off you, even if they are not in the room."

I laughed as we walked out of my room. "Father brings fear wherever he goes, even if he is not unhappy. It will be a long time before I can match that."

Nikalye chuckled again but said nothing. While he did not fear Father, and neither did I because I knew he would never hurt me, Nikalye would always understand why no one spoke ill of him.

"He will fear you one day, *mi Belleza Oscura*." He pressed the button on my lift so that it came back up.

"Where are we going?" I did not want to go into the lesson, I was sure Nikalye knew this.

"We are going to the gates to welcome your father."

"He is coming?" I said it with a smile. It had been a long time since I had seen Father.

Nikalye nodded, his face lighting up just as mine had no doubt done. Nikalye loved to see me happy. I squeezed his hand as my lift opened. We stepped inside, and Nikalye pressed the button to go down.

"You should have put shoes on, *mi Belleza Oscura*," Nikalye said with a frown, looking at my bare feet.

I looked also. "Walking bare footed does not bother me, do not worry." My lift opened and we walked out into the empty common room and outside. There was hardly any breeze and the air around us was considerably warm. We headed through the trees, following a path marked by scattered small stones. I did not mind walking bare footed on the stones. They did not hurt me in the slightest. I knew Nikalye wanted to say something to me, maybe even offer to carry me, but I had told him that I was fine without shoes and if I was bothered, he knew I would tell him so.

As we walked in silence through the trees, ducking under low branches, my thoughts strayed to Shade. He was all I could think about lately. I should be annoyed with that because I did not really know him and already I had kissed him on more than just his lips.

What I would like to understand is why I could not stop thinking about him, his touch, taste and the way he made me feel with his eyes alone.

"*Mi Belleza Oscura*, there is an answer to everything, no matter how hard the question is."

"Nikalye, it is not polite to intrude into ones thoughts." I smiled.

"*Mi Belleza Oscura*, I was not intruding into your thoughts, you were merely shouting them, throwing them at me if you will."

I laughed. "I am sorry. I did not mean to throw such rudeness at you."

"Do not worry."

I said nothing as we continued to walk further into the thick of trees. "What is on your mind, *Guerrero?*" He was normally quite, but never with me. He always had something to say, a story, information, advice.

"I am thinking about you and Mr. Shade."

"What about us?" I glanced at him and saw that his face was a mask of concentration.

"What you were thinking about, *mi Belleza Oscura*, I was wondering the same thing."

"Why he makes me feel the way he does?"

"Indeed, as I said, there is an answer to everything, no matter how hard the question. I will find that answer."

"And I should hope you will tell me, yes?" I said with a smile.

Nikalye looked at me, also smiling. "I cannot keep anything from you."

"That is true," I said as the trees opened out into a small field with large, spiked black iron gates at the end. My heart began to beat faster and I couldn't help but smile as I watched the large gates open and Father walked through them with Doxiak close behind.

I broke into a run and in less than a second, I was in Father's arms. He held me tight, pressed a kiss into my hair before he held me at arm's length and looked at me with a smile.

"You are a beauty as ever. How are you?"

"I am coping," I answered, unable to give him any other

answer.

"I hope you are keeping yourself out of trouble."

I grinned. "Have you been keeping yourself out of trouble, Father?" I asked with one eyebrow raised. He laughed and pulled me into another hug.

"I have missed you."

"Me, too," I whispered. Father gave me a gentle squeeze.

"Come, show me your finished room, I have not seen it." We walked away, leaving Doxiak at the gates.

"Maybe you should visit more then." I raised my pierced eyebrow. Father clucked his tongue as he studied my face.

"Maybe I should, but was it not you who did not want me seeing you the way you were?"

"Maybe so, but you are my father. You should not have listened to me."

Father laughed loudly, the sound echoing around the trees, making the birds nearby fly away with a loud beat of wings. I watched some of them go, flying into the distance where the mountains were until they were nothing more than dots.

"What have you done so far in your lessons?" Father asked as we walked.

"How do you know I started my lessons?" I wondered.

"I informed him, *mi Belleza Oscura*," Nikalye told me with a slight smile as he looked at my Father.

They were lifelong friends. Father taught Nikalye how to fight when he was just a boy and when he learned about Nikalye's visions, when Nikalye was much older, he wanted him as a guard. Nikalye accepted and they had been friends ever since. Though Nikalye was now a guard for Master Tyroz, he and Father spoke regularly.

Since I came back, he and Father had not been able to see much of each other because of me and guilt washed through me because of that. It was true that I did not want Father seeing me at my worst, did not want him hearing me scream when the nightmares of my memories took over or struggle to cope with my hunger as it burned through me, torturing me. Though I did not cry through it all, Nikalye knew how much I was hurting and so did Father.

"*Mi Belleza Oscura*, you should not feel guilty, you did not want him to see you as you were, that's understandable." Nikalye murmured in Spanish.

"But does he understand?" I replied in the favored language.

"I understand everything about my daughter," Father said in Spanish, shocking me into looking at him. He stopped in his tracks and stood in front of me, his hands on my shoulders. "You should know that I know everything about you by now. I knew how you were feeling because I have felt exactly the same at some point in my life, though for different reasons."

"I am sorry, Father. I should have known," I spoke quietly while looking down. Father lifted my face up and made me look at him.

"You do not need to be sorry, daughter. You have been through something no vampire, not even I could survive. You are entitled to forget a few important things."

"Liar," I murmured with a smile. "You are the strongest, most fearless vampire I have ever met and I am privileged to have you as a father. You can survive through anything."

"That is true, but some things even I cannot survive." He hugged me and kissed the top of my head, stopping me from calling him a liar once more. "Come, now is not the time to dwell in the past." He let me go and turned around with a smile on his face. Nikalye took my hand, also smiling, and pulled me forward, following my father.

"Your Father learned to speak Spanish when we brought you back."

"That was around the time when you and Father spoke alone with each other while I needed space?" I asked.

"Yes," Nikalye replied. He did not need to elaborate because I remembered clearly. I spoke only in Spanish instead of English fluently because I was afraid and knew only Nikalye could understand. I needed my privacy, but I did not want to be alone and speaking in a different tongue was the only way I could get such privacy.

"So, daughter, tell me what you have learned so far," Father said, pulling me out of my own thoughts.

"Nothing I do not already know, Father. You taught me well."

He chuckled a little. "That is not what I hear. I hear that you fought a young man and he knocked you to the floor."

"I am not unbeatable," I replied.

"Oh, I know that, but what I cannot understand is why you would let anyone beat you."

"He is an incredible fighter, Father. You should see him, even you would be amazed," I said it with a smile as I remembered how skilfully he moved around the room.

"But he also is not unbeatable, my daughter. I expect you to show him how well I have taught you. How well you can be in control."

I smiled widely, remembering clearly how Shade reacted when I was in control. "Do not worry, Father. When I am in control, he does not know how to handle the situation," I said as the memories of him groaning and gripping my hair tight as I took him into my mouth flitted through my mind.

"*Mi Belleza Oscura*—" Nikalye said, choking on a laugh.

I looked at him with wide eyes when he started laughing, doubled over and clutching his stomach. Even I could not help the smile that spread across my face at the sight. Nikalye had not laughed this much in years.

"What is wrong?" Father asked, also coming to a stop.

I glanced at him, grateful of the fact that he could not read minds like Nikalye could.

"He is losing it, Father," I said solemnly, shaking my head and hiding my smile easily.

Father shook his head and he could not help but smile as Nikalye stood and straightened his clothes, not a smile in sight.

"You are fine now?" Father asked.

Nikalye looked at me and I saw his eyes flash as he nodded. Father turned and walked away. I followed when Nikalye was by my side.

"I am sorry, *Guerrero*. I did not mean for that to happen."

"Do not worry, *mi Belleza Oscura*. I am just not used to stepping into your thoughts when you are thinking so...intimately. I am used to your thoughts being dark, in shadows."

"I am still sorry. No one should see anything like that." Nikalye squeezed my hand, but said nothing as we walked out of the trees and across the grass. As we walked, the doors to the living accommodations opened and before I could even look at Father, he had disappeared. I blew out a breath until I saw Shade walk out of the building. His eyes locked onto mine instantly before he glanced at Nikalye's and my fingers laced together. When he met my eyes again, he raised his eyebrows.

"Master Nikalye." He bowed his head respectfully.

"Young Shade, you are well?" Nikalye squeezed my hand, telling me that he had not missed anything that passed between Shade and I.

"I am, and yourself?"

"I am fine."

I slipped my hand out of Nikalye's and took a step toward Shade. "I need to speak to Shade, about what he knows and what he should not do," I told Nikalye.

"That would be a wise thing to do," Nikalye said. "We will be in your room," he added in Spanish.

"Okay." In Spanish, I added, "Explain what I'm doing please."

Nikalye nodded and placed a kiss on the top of my head before he nodded his head to Shade and walked away. I watched him go before I turned to Shade.

"Is there anywhere we can go?" I asked.

He nodded and walked toward the training building. I walked close behind, following him into the building and into the training hall. Shade held the door on the other side of the room open for me and then we walked into the room where I had my trial run. He shut the door behind us and I opened my mouth to speak, but Shade pulled me into his arms and captured my lips in a kiss so hungry, my legs went weak instantly. I moaned into his mouth, running my fingers into his hair so I could pull him closer. He moved, ending our kiss and I felt the wall at my back before his lips were at my neck and his hands were under my top, making my skin heat up as his hands flexed on my hips. I moaned, gripping his muscled arms tightly before I ran my fingers down them and slipped my hands under his top, over the rippling muscles across his stomach and to his chest.

There was a noise outside, making Shade lift his head from my neck. I took a deep breath and then I heard the footsteps coming from outside the door. I looked at Shade quickly, opening my mouth to speak when he kissed me again and then pulled me across the room. Halfway across, something cold washed over me, making me shiver slightly before Shade was kissing me again. I turned my head, gasping in a breath before I spoke.

"They will see us regardless of the fact that we are across the room."

Shade chuckled, turned me around in his arms and

pushed me up against the wall. "We are in a hologram, Little Dhampir. They will not be able to see us," he said as he ground himself against me.

I moaned a little and pushed myself against him, feeling his erection pressed against my backside. He groaned and I moaned when he slipped his hand easily down my shorts, thrusting his fingers into me and making pleasure shoot through me.

"They will only be able to hear us."

He breathed into my ear as he lifted one of my legs up, opening me wider to his touch. I dropped my head back onto his shoulders and moaned loudly as he slipped his fingers out of me and ran them over my clitoris, wetting it with his slick fingers.

The door to the hall opened and Shade stopped pleasuring me as three vampires, two males and a female I had not yet met walked in, shutting the door behind them. They took a few steps away from the door, but that was all they did.

"This room is used for trials and such, to test the vampires on their speed, strength and knowledge…"

I gasped a little as Shade moved his fingers. He turned my head toward him and kissed me hard. The pleasure inside me, the hunger—for both blood and him—rose quickly once more. I was going to come and it would be soon if Shade did not stop. Those vampires would be able to hear.

I knew I would not care.

"Shade—" I moaned a little as he pushed himself against me and thrust his fingers inside.

"Shh," he whispered with a grin.

I growled a little and spun around in his arms, pushing him to the floor. I rode his fingers as though it were his erection and stifled my moans in the fabric of his top.

"The students here are eager to learn, especially after the trial. I think there was only one student who has managed to fully complete the trial and there was no surprise there, seeing as she is the daughter of—"

The man stopped speaking when I gasped loudly with pleasure as Shade rubbed my clitoris. It would have turned into a cry of pleasure if Shade had not locked his lips with mine to stop it.

"Come, we have business to talk," the female vampire said, getting the two males' attention as she walked over and opened the door. She waited for the two vampires to pass before walking out, shutting the door behind her. As soon as she did so, Shade spun around, pinning me to the floor and rubbed my clitoris harder. I exploded instantly, arching off the floor and crying out with pleasure loudly, the sound echoed off the walls around the room. I burned, my body heated and aching for more than just Shade's fingers. My body longed for him to be inside me—filling me, stretching me and pleasuring me repeatedly.

Shade kissed me hungrily, catching my cries as I came again. I grabbed his wrist, but he was too strong for me and I could not move him. I wrapped my legs around him and pulled him into me, making him growl against my lips as his erection rubbed against my hand. I gasped for breath, trying to fight the pleasure, but Shade did not give me chance to. He continued to rub me as he reached the top of my shorts to pull them down.

"Protection…" I gasped wildly. Shade stilled, both the hand on my shorts and the one on my clitoris, though it did not stop the pleasure from rising even though he had done so.

"Damn," he stopped touching me all together with both his hands.

I could not help a little moan escaping me at the loss.

"Sorry, Little Dhampir, but if I do not stop touching you now, I will not stop." He kissed me gently before getting to his feet, pulling me along with him.

I closed my eyes, taking a deep calm breath, knowing Shade was watching me do so before we both walked out of the hall. The vampires here before were nowhere to be seen so it was easy for us to walk through the training hall and outside without being seen.

"Shade, I wanted to talk to you about me," I said as we walked across the grass. I tilted my head toward the darkness as a cold breeze blew across my face, making my slightly damp skin break out in goose bumps.

"What about you?"

"About me being a dhampir and you knowing about it."

"Don't worry, your secret is safe with me. I am not going to tell anyone. I promise."

I breathed a sigh of relief as Shade opened the door to the living accommodations. I knew I could trust Shade not to tell anyone, though I did not know why. I hardly knew him.

"Nikalye is waiting in my room for me, I cannot keep him waiting any longer than I have done so. He will begin to worry." Shade kissed my lips once and then smiled.

"I'll see you tomorrow."

He kissed me again, harder this time and slid his tongue into my mouth. I moaned a little and growled when he caught his tongue on my fang and I tasted his blood. I sucked on his tongue almost hungrily, making him groan before he stepped away from me. I let him with my eyes shut because of the hunger burning through me. I took another deep breath before I turned away without a word and walked to my lift. Shade did not call me back, but let me go. I knew his eyes were on me as I waited for my lift and it was only when it opened and I stepped inside that I looked at him, just as my lift doors shut.

I blew out a breath and leaned against the wall as it took me up. When it opened, I walked straight into my bathroom so I could freshen up and let the scent of both Shade's and my own arousal settle down before I walked into my bedroom.

Nikalye was leaned up against the wall, near the head of my bed, his hands held behind him. Father was nowhere where to be seen I until I saw that my wardrobe door was open.

"Mi Belleza Oscura?"

I looked at Nikalye and knew that he knew what happened between Shade and I. I did not worry as I knew Nikalye would not say a word.

"He has promised not to say a word," I said as Father came back into my room.

"And you trust the boy?" Father asked.

I nodded and smiled. "If my gut told me otherwise, Father, I would not trust him with anything."

"Ah yes, that gut of yours is incredibly accurate."

I laughed a little and watched as Father looked around my room. "Do you like it?" Though Father had gotten my bed, my chest and designed my wardrobe, he had not actually seen it all together.

"I have good taste," Father replied, causing me to laugh.

"*I* have good taste, Father. Not all of this was yours."

Father gave me a look before he smiled. "The room is as good as my daughter should have it. Though I do not know why you insist on having this much window." Father did not like the thought of the sun waking him up while he was sleeping. Though he was incredibly old and could go out in the sun without being irritated, he tended not to unless he had to.

"I am a dhampir, Father. I love the sun as much as the next dhampir."

"You are more than a dhampir, daughter."

"Indeed, but that does not change the fact that I like the sun, love it even, even if you do not." I walked up to him and hugged him, stopping him from saying anything more on the fact of what I was. "The sun cannot harm me, Father, and no one can get into my lift to see the fact that I have a window, let alone a large one. Do not worry."

"I always worry about my daughter's safely. You are the only thing I have left."

I squeezed him, feeling guilt and sadness wash through both of us. "You have Nikalye," I said, making him chuckle.

"This is very true."

I looked up at him and he smiled widely at me, all thoughts of the past gone.

"I must be going."

"When will you come back?"

"When I can." He kissed my forehead. "I love you, my daughter. Be safe."

"You, too."

He kissed my forehead once more before hugging me tight and leaving my room. Nikalye kissed the top of my head before smiling at me reassuringly.

"I will be back as soon as your father is out of the gates." He knew I would not come to say bye to Father. It was too hard for me to do so.

"Be careful, *Guerrero*."

He smiled before bowing and walking out of my room, closing the door behind him. The smile on my face slipped as soon as I was alone. I turned to look out of the window and saw the sun setting from behind the mountains. I knew this is why Father had to go. He may be strong enough to handle any dangers outside of the academy, but his guards waiting outside the gate for him — other than Doxiak — were not.

I looked away from the view as I sat on my chair and closed my eyes, feeling incredibly lonely.

Chapter Twelve

"Okay, so Master Nikalye has informed me that you have gone through the enemies' weapons and how they affect us." Everyone nodded.

I did not, I did not wish to speak to anyone in this class, I would only get mad. My mood was not considerably my best and wearing some of my favourite clothes, a black and red corset, black skinny jeans and black heeled boots, was not making me feel any better. I was hungry for blood I knew I could not have. I was hungry for the touch I knew I should not have. I was not very happy.

I did not think Diaxon or Nikalye could stop me when I was in one of my rages.

"So today we are going to be discussing why the enemies are doing what they are doing, why are they attacking us. Why are they capturing us and forcing us to hide. And while we are doing that, we will be combining your lesson with Raikez, if you will follow me." Diaxon walked across the hall to the door where I had my trial run. Nikalye walked by my side as we went up some stairs and into a large room at the top. There were already vampires seated in this room and the vampires from my group greeted them happily. I walked to the back and sat in the shadows. Shade stood next to Diaxon at the front. The class was now a class of thirty teenage vampires.

"Okay. Listen up." Raikez was a big and muscular

vampire, dressed in casual clothes. He looked like he could snap one of us in half with his little finger. "Quiet!"

Everyone stopped speaking as if someone pressed mute on a remote. I was slightly amused.

"Those of you who don't know, we have a new student to this academy." He gestured to the back of the room.

My amusement disappeared. I did not think I liked this vampire. I did not want anyone to notice me.

"Please stand and tell us who you are."

I glanced at Nikalye. He shook his head, not looking at me. I reluctantly stood and all eyes were on me in an instant. I looked at Shade, but only for half a second. I could see the heat in his eyes and I could feel my body reacting to that, wanting his touch.

"*Soy Layla,*" I sat down. My group, who knew I spoke in Spanish, erupted with amused talk and sniggering, some leaned over to explain to the others why they found it amusing until the man coughed and everyone fell silent.

"That isn't what I meant."

I raised my eyebrows, leaning back on my chair. I responded in Spanish, even though I knew he couldn't understand me, especially because Nikalye was not translating.

The vampire looked at Nikalye, and then at Diaxon. "She does not speak English?"

"She does when she wishes," Nikalye replied.

He looked at me and I knew he was getting annoyed.

"Stand please."

I stood, my temper raising a notch.

"What is your full name?"

"That is not relevant," Nikalye said from behind me.

The man looked irritated. "Tell me. How was the first vampire created?"

I smiled sweetly. He was trying to make me look like a

fool. I replied in Spanish.

"In English, *mi Belleza Oscura...*" Nikalye said with amusement.

"It was a human who has created the first vampire," I said in English.

"Elaborate, *mi Belleza Oscura...*" Nikalye said, making me smile.

I could tell he was trying not to laugh. He did not like the vampire as much as I did. "An Egyptian human created the first vampire. It was not called vampire back then, it was called *bloodsucker*. The man in question experimented on his best friend in the year sixteen forty-four. He trusted him very much so you can see why he killed him. The man injected his friend with a lot of silver and it burned his skin after many doses. He burned his friend with many of sun's rays, leaving him on the hot sand when the sun was at its highest, burning him severely before treating his wounds and doing it all over again. After weeks of doing this, his friend became very sensitive to both silver and sunlight. The slightest touch, the slightest exposure to sunlight and the man burned badly.

"That is not all he did because, you see, the Egyptian had possession over something powerful, something he should have read carefully before doing what he did, the Book of the Dead with pages that are full of spells and rituals. The man did several incantations on his friend. Two of those spells were able to help preserve the dead person's heart and the heart's role in re-unifying the dead person's body and soul and allowed a deceased to breathe once more. These were just two of the spells the man did. He did incantations hoping to preserve and reunite the human if he should die on the table.

"Only when a body is dead, should the spells be spoken, to preserve and reunite the persons being, as well as give him control over the world around him, not someone alive.

"So afterward, when the Egyptian had finished playing with the body, he wanted to take things further. I do not know how he could have possibly thought he could do anything worse than use spells on him. He injected him with a created mix he himself created from herbs, crushed healing stones and such—although he did not know if the mixture was safe or not—his best friend began to heal fast and his skin began to harden to the point that it was very hard to get a needle into his vein.

"He did not stop there, he experimented further and drained his friend of but a pint of blood and then put it all back in him. He did this repeatedly for days to see if there were any changes. It was after he cut his hand badly that he noticed that his friend craved the blood because you see, after draining him, the air took away the oxygen in the blood so when it was put back in, the man was suffocating. The man could smell the oxygen in the blood and wanted it.

"He tortured him beyond unbearable pain so when his friend broke free of his restraints, not only did he see that he was extremely strong and fast, but he saw the true monster he created." I stopped, for a dramatic pause.

"His friend killed his creator. He fled into the night where he fed on the veins of innocents and killed them all. He died soon after, but he had altered genes and the...*virus*, shall we call it, spread through his blood. When he attacked his own wife and bled her to the point of death, he realised what he had done and tried to make things right. He was not thinking when he put his own blood into his wife. She lost consciousness and when she next woke, her beloved husband, thinking he had killed her was nothing but a pile of ash on the floor. Thinking he had killed her with his contaminated blood, he had exposed himself to the sun's rays so he could be with his wife. What he did not know was that he had changed her instead.

"His wife did not know what he had become or what she had become. She fled and hid, but when hunger took over, she went crazy. She, unlike her husband, had a little sense and she did not kill the human whose vein she opened. The man was her best friend and he trusted her with anything. You think that humans would not make that same mistake of trusting their friends, but they were different. She was lonely and asked her friend if he wanted to become what she had so they could face the unknown together and help others. He agreed and that very night and he, too, became what she was.

"They lived in Egypt but it was hard. The sun was hot, even if the night was cool, but they did not like hiding during the day. They managed it, but they noticed that soon, years later after hiding for so long, they were not aging. This caused problems because people noticed. They had to flee from Egypt to another part of the world, where they would start all over again.

"They were very good bloodsuckers drinking only when they had to. They killed, yes, but not anyone who would have others missing them. This did not stop the humans from noticing however, and at first, they thought they were witches and chased them down. The bloodsuckers did not stay in one place for more than a couple of years. If anyone suspected them, they would flee once more. They made more along the way and the populations of humans went down while the bloodsuckers went up because where the widow and her friend were cautious, these new bloodsuckers were not. They killed anyone, caused destruction and mayhem. The humans were very smart and they suspected what was wrong. They hunted them all down, found their weakness and used that against them.

"However, when the humans cornered the widow, her

best friend, and their new *family*, a human rescued them. This was unheard of and they could not be sure if they could really trust this beautiful woman. They killed her kindly by stabbing her through the heart. She was only a small woman. She died instantly, but with a smile on her face. They fled from the woman's corpse, but they met her again, in her spirit form. She told them what she was—a Spirit Demon. She told them that she did not blame them for what they did. She knew about the humans hunting them.

"The other Spirit Demons did not take kindly to what they did. The woman told them to give the bloodsuckers another chance to prove themselves. They agreed, but they had to understand that they could not make others like themselves because like us, the Spirit Demons needed the humans to live to survive.

"However, we are not dead, the women could get pregnant and the genes spread to their young. The vampires born would be very strong, quick and heal fast. Their bodies also adapted to the change that happened to their parents and their canines were longer, sharper, great for biting and feeding on blood. The Spirit Demon and the vampire also had a child."

This got the class whispering.

"Others fell in love with humans who did not know what they were. They had to leave their loved ones behind, but took with them a child. A child that took on more traits of the vampire than human, say like the fangs and the thirst for blood. The child was not a vampire, it was half-human, half-vampire. They are known as dhampirs."

The class laughed loudly.

"What vampire would sink that low?" Lohron asked.

I narrowed my eyes as I looked at him.

"You forget, Lohron, most of the original vampires fell in love with humans. It is not a crime," Nikalye said, obviously sensing my anger.

"It should be against the laws. Dhampirs are not vampires. They aren't as strong or fast."

"And yet—" I said loudly and irritably.

"Layla—" Both Nikalye and Diaxon warned at the same time.

"You had a dhampir put you on the floor in less than a second," I finished, ignoring them both.

Everyone stayed silent. For a second at most...

"You're a dhampir?"

Chapter Thirteen

" And one that can put you on the floor," I reminded him once more. He didn't like that.

"So your dad just fell in love with a human?" Lohron asked.

I looked at him and did not answer.

"Your dad must be pretty low if he fucked one."

I was across the room before anyone saw me move, a blur too fast for their eyes. Only one saw me, but even he could not get to me as I twisted Lohron's arm behind his back and pushed his face into his table. Everyone who did not know me, jumped back. They did not know what to do. This was fine by me.

I put my lips close to Lohron's ear and pushed his wrist back. I knew he was in pain and I knew I could snap his wrist if I wanted. "You do not know my father. It is not wise to mock him as you do." I squeezed the back of his neck and twisted his wrist further.

"Little Dhampir," Shade's voice was gentle but with warning.

Nikalye and Diaxon stood not far from him, ready to take action if it went further.

"Be thankful your friends are here to save you. Should you have been alone, I would be drinking your blood while you died slowly in my arms. It is not a nice way to go. Cross me carefully from now on." I squeezed his neck, drawing a little blood and then walked away, back to my corner with Nikalye behind me and Shade watching me go.

Raikez was the first to react. He cleared his throat and then looked at Diaxon. He did not know how to handle a situation like this. He did not like violence even for a vampire.

"Continue with your lesson," he told Raikez.

Shade finally looked away.

"Erm, yes, Layla is correct in what she has told us. It was indeed the humans that created the first vampire, but he was killed."

"So, would you like to tell the class why the humans are hunting us, Mr. Khilorh?" Diaxon asked.

Everyone looked at Shade.

"They don't know that they were the ones that created us, they think we just rose from the dead, seeking revenge. They think we are creatures of Satan. They are threatened by us and the only way they know how to deal with it is by fighting."

"Very good, yes, though, as Miss Layla told you, it was indeed the humans who created us out of a selfish need to be someone. The very thing he created killed him. When the new vampire attacked his wife, the memories of all his suffering transferred to her, which is how she knew she was not human. When the humans caught on to the fact that there were vampires — or bloodsuckers — living among them, they knew nothing about who created us, only what they believe.

"Now, they caught on fairly quickly as to what we were because — apart from the widow and her best friend — the vampires were not born with coloured skin and we were living among the tanned skinned humans. No one would see us during the day, only at night, and people were disappearing. We were not stealthy creatures back then and because we were not aging, we had to move around. On and on we went to different places all over the world. Hiding, feeding and coming to terms about what we were. It was when a vampire stumbled upon a mugging and snapped the mugger's spine in half that people saw they were different, not human. The woman who saw ran before anyone could stop her and soon all the vampires were chased away from their homes by fire.

"Now, even back then there were stories going around, myths, about someone who was cursed to eternity into drinking human blood to survive, a demon that enjoyed the killings. After seeing what the vampire could do and how effortless it was to do so, the humans based them around that demon. It is when they started calling them *bloodsuckers*. They learned quickly what to look for. Any pale-skinned people had sharp wooden sticks driven through their hearts. This killed the humans they thought were bloodsuckers instantly, but only wounded the vampires, causing them to go into a state of death. As soon as the stake was out of their flesh and blood was force fed to them, they healed quickly. The humans noticed this, too, and decided that maybe wood was not the way to go. It was then they turned to silver. Something they did not have much of, but that was a small sacrifice to rid the world of evil."

With the little silver they had, they would melt it and make weapons, short daggers, swords and even arrowheads, stuff they could use repeatedly. They killed many vampires with those weapons and today they have upgrades.

"Now, you know about the widow and her best friend. They travelled everywhere together, never leaving each other's side, always protecting each other. They were smart enough to flee when the attacks started. Most vampires were not and they died painfully. The widow and her best friend always looked over their shoulders. If they saw a human, they would hide. When they needed to feed, they would not kill, they would knock them out before cutting them and drinking. So, just as Layla said, when they were cornered by a bunch of humans, and a beautiful female saved them, the widow's best friend, despite the fact that she was human, fell in love with her. This is because she was very beautiful in his eyes, very strong and someone worthy enough to handle what he was.

"But they could not allow themselves to fall in love with the very things that were hunting them down. This is why the widow killed her while her best friend walked away. As Layla already informed you, she was not human, she was a Spirit Demon, Surquyn Ramlie, Queen Surquyn Ramlie, who the widow killed and, as you know, she came back and found them. She explained who she was, what she was and told them that they had nothing to fear from her. Now, the other Spirit Demons did not like the bloodsuckers like Queen Surquyn did, but because she was Queen, they did not harm them, instead, can anyone tell me what they did to help the bloodsuckers?"

No one said a word. Diaxon looked at me and raised his eyebrows.

"They helped build a safe place on these hundred acres of land so that the vampires had somewhere safe away from the humans to live," I said. Everyone looked at me but did not say a word. They obviously did not want to anger a dhampir.

"And was this a good thing or bad?" Diaxon asked.

I shrugged. "Both good and bad, it depends on how you look at it."

"Elaborate..." Nikalye murmured quietly.

"It was good, because after a while, the humans stopped looking for us and our numbers went up. It was bad, because the vampires got into disagreements. Fights broke out and some were killed."

"What else?" Diaxon asked.

"The Shadow Demons made themselves known."

"Shadow Demons?" Arezon asked.

"Do you know what a Shadow Demon is?" Diaxon asked. She shook her head and he looked at me, nodding.

"Shadow Demons are very much alive, though they have no form. It is Shadow Demons that hover around this academy, making sure nothing gets in, and no one gets out."

"But I heard Shadow Demons are bad," Kalitha said.

"They are, in some sense, yes. Some vampires would hunt them because by drinking the blood of a Shadow Demon, you gain a part of their soul. Most vampires strive for power and died painfully."

"Why?" Niaxoz asked.

I looked at him for a couple of seconds before answering. "Most Shadow Demons are evil, they feed on the despair that comes from the humans like oxygen. When they found out that there was a new creature in existence, ones who fed from the humans, drinking their blood, they began to hunt vampires down, for fun as well as to feed. The vampires enjoyed the thought of being able to become the shadow. It is in all vampires to want power that is not theirs. As I said, they hunted them down and drank their blood. In some sense, it does make them more powerful, but it also poisons them. The Shadow feeds of the life force of humans so when the vampire drinks their blood, whatever life force they have — say, the human oxygen running through their veins — the vampires starve and die in a matter of seconds as the oxygen is sucked away. It is a waste of an act to do such thing. But there will always be some who think they are stronger and they will survive."

"Why did all of that stop, Layla?" Diaxon asked.

"The humans began attacking again. They never really

thought we were out of existence and throughout the years, they planned and passed down their knowledge to their sons and their sons sons. They began forming a group with weapons no man has ever come across. Weapons specially designed to knock us down. Not kill us. Everyone came to an agreement once the humans started to attack, no one, Spirit, vampire or Shadow can attack one another."

"Good and last but not least. Can you tell me why they wanted weapons to capture us and not kill us?"

"To experiment on us, to see how our bodies work. To experiment, just as the human did to his best friend and inject humans with the blood of vampires, werewolves, shifters, demons and angels."

"They inject their own kind? You would think they would have learned," Leidon said, making Berlox and some others around him snigger.

"If they had known that it was indeed they who created us in the first place, I am sure they would have," I said to Leidon. The room was taking in every word I was saying, even though I was a dhampir. "But they didn't, and they became curious as to what they could create. They thought that by injecting humans with the blood of a vampire, of a wolf and other creatures, they could create creatures that can destroy us once and for all."

"These humans are called Mutated," Diaxon said. This got everyone whispering to each other.

"So they thought they could get rid of us by creating something that's stronger than them?" Leidon asked.

"Correct."

"But why can't we just find that Spirit Demon, vampire kid? I'm sure that can help us," Lohron asked.

"Because she is dead," Diaxon replied simply.

"Damn, if we had a half-Spirit Demon, half-vampire, we'd have no problem stopping the humans from attacking us."

"What makes you think she could have helped?" I asked.

Lohron turned to look at me. "Because she's like the ultimate creature. She can drain people dry, walk out into the sunlight and basically be human. They wouldn't even see her coming."

"You were so quick to put me down, Lohron. Why not put this creature down?"

"That's different, you drink vampire blood."

"And you think she wouldn't?" I asked.

"She couldn't, she's a vampire."

"A Spirit Demon is human," I countered. That threw him off. He frowned as he looked at me, pondering my words.

He turned to Diaxon. "Would she drink human or vampire blood?"

He shrugged. "No one knows. She was a secret, until now. All I know is that she was very powerful."

Lohron glanced at me again before looking back at Diaxon.

Raikez spoke before Diaxon could. "Right until the humans captured her that is."

Chapter Fourteen

"**W**hat? The humans caught her?" Lohron asked as everyone gasped in shock.

"Indeed," Diaxon replied.

Lohron shook his head in disbelief. "What happened?"

"No one fully knows," Raikez replied. "There were whispers, whispers that are still going around, whispers about how the humans broke into her home while she slept and dragged her out of bed. They drove off with her as her mother and father arrived, and a big fight broke out. Queen Surquyn was killed in battle."

"Shit."

"Very much so, the spirit girl's father tracked her down, killing any human that got in his way with rage until he found her."

"She was dead?" Arezon asked, captivated by the story just as everyone else was, unlike me.

"She was found cut open, emptied of blood —"

I drowned out the sound of his voice. I did not want to listen to something I already knew. I looked at Nikalye when he touched my arm gently. He gestured for me to stand and follow him across the room and out into the hall.

"I know you do not like to hear this story."

"I do not, no."

"But they need to know this."

I said nothing. I did not even look at him.

"Layla."

"There is nothing to say, Master Nikalye," I replied as the door opened and Diaxon walked into the hallway.

"*Mi Belleza Oscura*, how can I help you if you will not talk?"

I took a deep calming breath. "I am hungry."

He said nothing for a while. Diaxon also did not speak, but he did exchange a look with Nikalye.

"I will contact Master Tyroz. I will have him come here once this lesson has finished. I will discuss the matter beforehand. He will want to meet the young vampires and see how you are doing."

I nodded. "Thank you."

"You may go to your room. I will tell Raikez that this lesson is going to be cut short," Diaxon said.

I shook my head. "I will stay for the remainder of the lesson. I do not want to be treated differently."

"Very well," he replied.

"I will be back shortly to escort everyone from this lesson," Nikalye said, kissing the top of my head. He opened the door for me.

I smiled as I walked past him into the room. I met Shade's eyes and looked away quickly. Talking about being hungry made me hungrier and looking at Shade was making my body react in many ways.

"Ladies and gentlemen, I am afraid that we can only continue this lesson for a couple more minutes. We will be having a visit from Master Tyroz."

Everyone in the class began to murmur. I opened my eyes, saw Shade get up and make his way to me. Lohron and his other friends watched him.

"Little Dhampir."

"Shade." He took a seat next to me.

"What is wrong?"

"How do you know anything is wrong?" I asked curiously. I looked into his eyes. If he were lying, I would know in an instant.

"You are not easily provoked. Yet Lohron did that in just a second."

"He spoke poorly of my father. I love my father."

"Yes, I understand that, but you reacted badly. You told him in front of a class of witnesses that had his friends not been there, you would have drained him dry. Not only did you give away that you are a dhampir who drinks vampire blood, but you lost control because of your hunger."

"I did not lose control."

"What would have happened if no one, but Lohron and you were here?"

I did not answer. He knew what I would have done. I could see that in his eyes. I would have bitten him and I would have drained him dry while he struggled against me.

"Why do you care?" I settled on saying. It was a horrible thing to say because I knew he cared even more than he realised, just as I did him. Shade searched my face.

"I care a lot more than you think."

"Why? I am nothing more than a dhampir who likes to drain vampires dry." I stood quickly and my chair toppled back. The room went quiet and everyone looked at me.

"Layla, if you please."

I glared at Diaxon before walking across the room. I walked out while he was speaking with Raikez. He caught up to me easily as I began to walk down the curved stairs.

"I am going to get some fresh air," I said calmly.

"Do you wish me to escort you?"

"I am fine," I stopped at the doors and looked at Diaxon. "Thank you for staying calm when I was not."

"You were quite calm."

"Yes, considering," I said, looking past Diaxon to see the

others, escorted by Raikez, walk into the hall.

"I will come when Master Tyroz has arrived."

Diaxon smiled before walking toward them.

I walked away, going outside and across the grass slowly. The air was cold, but it did not bother me. I looked up, closing my eyes and just let it breeze across my face, calming me down.

I knew it was a foolish thing to do, revealing who I was. I did not know how Master Tyroz would react to that news, especially because I threatened one of his people. I did not want to think about how Father would react. I hated to see him angry.

I heard the murmur of voices, but did not bother looking around. I knew who it was and they did not say anything to disturb me. I knew they were glancing at me, that they knew who and what I was.

"Layla."

I opened my eyes and turned to Diaxon.

He bowed his head before standing straight with his hands clasped behind his back. "Master Tyroz is waiting for you in the hall."

I nodded and followed him across the grass.

"He is going to speak to you and then will decide if you can be trusted with drinking the blood of his people."

We stepped into the building. Diaxon stood behind me as I walked down the hall. We stopped when we got to the door. I could hear voices and something growling.

"They know not to address me by my title?" I asked, not looking at Diaxon.

"Yes. They know how important it is for you to remain a secret. They will address you as Layla."

I opened the door and walked into the hall. The first person I saw was Shade. He was standing with everyone but not interacting. He looked over and, as our eyes met, his gaze sent shivers down my spine.

I looked away and noticed a large golden brown lion—an angry lion judging by the fact that he was growling—in the middle of the hall surrounded by many guards.

Tyroz, tall and muscular with long black-brown hair, black eyes and lethal looking, was standing not far away. He seemed unsure of what to do. He did not want to frighten the teenagers by angering the lion further. Nikalye was standing with his arms folded across his muscular chest in the shadows.

I walked across the hall and pushed my way to the lion. I was not afraid of it, having been in this situation before and besides, I was angry. If the lion wished to fight me, I did not mind. I would like the challenge. I grabbed the lion's mane and leaned close to his ear.

"Shifter, you should control your anger. One would think you are hiding something if you shift at everything that is said." I was merely guessing that someone had said something to upset him.

The lion growled and nudged my hand, then let out a snort.

I was right. I let go of him and walked toward Tyroz. Diaxon stood by the door and held it open while Shifter— still in his lion form—walked out.

"My thanks," Tyroz said once I reached him.

I nodded and looked at Nikalye.

"Mi Belleza Oscura."

I smiled and reverted to Spanish. "Hello, Nikalye."

He kept to our language. "How are you feeling?"

"Better thank you," I replied. He nodded and his gaze travelled down my body slowly.

"You look good enough to eat."

I laughed at his words and shook my head. Master Tyroz could speak Spanish of course and Nikalye enjoyed annoying him just a little with his words.

"Layla, how are your training lessons?" Tyroz interrupted before we could carry on. He did not look angry to see me, but he did not look calm either, which did not surprise me. He was always worried I would go on another rampage. He worried about the safety of his people more than my own. This did not bother me. Tyroz had never really cared for me as Nikalye had. To him, I was a half-breed he had to respect because he respected my father completely, though he would protect me as much as the next vampire would if I was in danger.

"They are fine so far," I replied.

"I have been informed that you are…stronger than a good deal of your class. Who bruised your hip?"

I looked down at my bare hip and at the slight colouring in my tanned skin. Though it did not look like anything was there, Tyroz had very good eyesight. I looked behind me and pointed to Shade. Tyroz looked, too, and then nodded with satisfaction. He obviously thought Shade was a worthy opponent.

"How have you been?" I asked politely.

"I have been fine. Nikalye has told me about your feeding requirements." He looked me up and down and then looked into my eyes. "Who have you tasted recently?" He said it in a low voice so no one could hear. I was grateful.

"Shade," I replied. I did not lie to him because he could smell a lie as he could smell fresh blood. It would not be wise to do so. He glanced at Shade and beckoned him over. I did not sense him move but suddenly, before I could turn around, he was by my side.

"You willingly let Layla sample your blood?" he asked Shade, his voice low and hard, but not threatening in the slightest.

"Yes, sir."

I looked at him as he spoke, he was calm, something most vampires were not when they were faced with Tyroz. Tyroz stared at Shade for a couple of seconds before glancing at me.

"You need to be careful, Layla. Your father will not be pleased if he finds out."

I nodded. "I can handle Father."

"I have to discuss this with Nikalye. I will call you over once I am finished." He did not wait for a reply, never did, just walked away.

"He took that better than I expected," Shade said as we walked away.

I leaned against the wall and Shade stood not far from me. "Yes, he did. That is not always a good thing." I sighed, watching Tyroz speaking to Nikalye. There was no doubt in my mind that Nikalye would try and sort out me being fed, even if it meant drinking from his vein, but I could see the worry on his face. Just like Tyroz, Nikalye saw me, but unlike Tyroz, Nikalye had seen the worst side of me and he wished nothing more than to help me heal, something we both knew he could not probably achieve.

I turned my attention to Shade when he stepped close to me and put his hands either side of my head. I looked up at him and felt my heart beat fast. He was very close to me, close enough that I could feel the heat coming off his body. Close enough that if I rose on my tip toes, our lips would touch —

"*Mi Belleza Oscura.*"

I looked around at the sound of Nikalye's voice. He was watching me with curiosity as well as concern. It was then that I realised everyone in the room was watching us, including Tyroz, Diaxon and Shifter, who was back in his human form.

"I'm fine, I replied in Spanish.

He answered in the same, "You're sure?"

"Please distract the others for me."

Nikalye nodded and walked toward the other vampires. I watched him distract the others as I asked as Shade spoke.

"Why did Nikalye teach you Spanish?"

"He prefers to speak Spanish?" I asked, smiling a little.

"You know what I mean," Shade said seriously.

I sighed a little. "Nikalye has been in my life right from the beginning. He looked after me when I needed it most and is still doing so today." It was not easy for him, but he managed it. We both knew I would not be as I used to be.

"Why, what happened to you?"

Anger surged through me at the thought. Nikalye was by my side in a second.

"Maybe you should stand with Diaxon," he told Shade.

"Nikalye, I am fine," I said, placing my hand on his arm.

"You are angered, *mi Belleza Oscura*."

I rubbed his arm. "It was nothing he did. I am just thinking about *The Mansion*. You know how it angers me to think about that time."

"Why do you think about it?"

"It is not easy to forget. You saw what happened. Have you forgotten?"

"I could never forget."

"See. It happened to me. You only saw through your eyes and you cannot forget. Do not worry. I am strong, you know that." Nikalye looked at me. He knew I was not lying and that was why he turned and walked away. I looked at Shade as he spoke.

"What happened?"

I looked away. If I lied to him, I knew that he would know in a second, just as I knew with him. "It is something that I cannot share lightly. Nikalye does not even know the full story. He just knows what he saw. It was how he found me he cannot forget." Shade looked at me.

He was very serious. "This is why he shadows you and you seek him when he is not there."

I nodded. He had guessed correctly so I saw no need to lie to him.

"Layla."

I looked at Tyroz before walking over to him. Shade stayed where he was. I could feel his gaze on my back, watching me.

"We are going to discuss the matter further. I will be in touch," Tyroz said.

I nodded and smiled. It was forced, I was hungry and I knew something was going to happen before I got blood.

"It was nice meeting you again." He bowed his head and walked away. I looked at Shade before walking away. The others, noticing that I was leaving, looked at me. I looked at Shifter. "Next time I see you, I hope you are not angry."

Shifter laughed, tall like the others with multi coloured hair, brown, black, yellow and red. His skin was tinged gold, just like my own, though for different reasons. He had a square jaw and full lips. His eyes were multi-coloured, just like his hair.

"Same to you, young Layla."

I smiled and turned to Nikalye. He offered me his arm and I took it, walking with him out of the building. The air was cool and the wind strong. I liked the cold as much as I liked the heat. I liked to train in the cold. I had to train harder in the cold than I did the heat, though the cold did not bother me in the slightest.

"Nikalye it is always a pleasure to see you." I knew Nikalye was going to leave.

"The pleasure's all mine. Goodbye, my Dark Beauty."

"Bye, Nikalye." I watched him go, thinking that I should to do something to get some steam off my chest. Once he had gone, I went back into the building. I was surprised to see all of the teenagers that were in the lesson standing on one side of the hall. I had expected them to have gone elsewhere, not look around as I walked in, as if they were waiting for me. I could hear them whispering excitedly. I caught Shade's eye and frowned. He walked up to me with a smile on his face. Lohron and a couple of others followed, but stayed a few feet away when Shade reached me. I was glad, I had no wish to listen to Lohron talking as I was still angry with him.

"What are you guys doing here?"

"The other group has heard about us fighting, they wish to see us fight with weapons. Our group, they want to see you get beaten again."

I smiled. "Hand-to-hand we are evenly matched. You only won because you used my body against me."

Shade smiled, showing fangs. "Weapons, I am not so sure. I am very good with my weapons."

"I guess there is only one way to find out."

Chapter Fifteen

I walked away to the weapons while Shade walked up to the others. I picked up two long bamboo sticks and handed Shade his before walking into the middle of the hall. Shade attacked when my back was turned. I turned away from his blow, twirling my stick in my hands. I swung and hit him on the back of his legs. He went down, but managed to turn around and knock my feet from underneath me. I rolled as soon as I hit the floor the same time Shade flipped himself to his feet. He swung his stick and I raised mine to block before blocking his next blow. I spun around on the floor with my leg sticking out and knocked him to the floor. I backed away before he could attempt to trip me again.

"Fifty she wins in less than a second when he gets up," Leidon said loudly. Some of the others from my group agreed and no one from the other group said anything, though they could not keep the surprise and amazement from their faces.

"A hundred she can't fight more than one of us," Lohron said as Shade got to his feet. He did not attack as I raised my eyebrows, liking that challenge.

"I'm in on that one," Shade said. "Only I bet that Little Dhampir *does* win."

"I second that," Arezon said.

I glanced at Shade and raised my eyebrows once more. "Fine, choose your best. Not that it will help," I said to

Lohron. He nudged some vampires and they all walked across the room to get their own weapons. I counted seven vampires, Leidon, Berlox, Gutax, Eailek, Tianshuk and two other males that I did not know from the other group.

"You are not really a fight," I said.

"You aren't just fighting me though, you're fighting seven of us as well as Shade," Lohron said.

"Hmm, I am still pretty confident," I said.

"Why don't you prove it?" Tianshuk said.

"Yeah, we'll be nice and we'll let you have the first hit," Lohron said, making me smile.

"That would be a very stupid thing to do."

"And why would that be?"

I moved fast and hit Lohron's hand, knocking his stick free. I swung my stick low, hit his legs, knocking him on the floor before I straightened up and caught the stick.

"Because I have your weapon," I said. I twisted my stick around in my hands and hit Leidon, Gutax and Eailek before kicking one of the vampires I didn't know in the face. Berlox and Tianshuk rushed at me, but I jumped in the air and kicked them both in the face before I landed and dropped down as someone kicked me from behind. I hit the legs of all of the vampires surrounding me and threw one of the sticks at Gutax, causing him to drop his own stick while I kicked another and then twisted around, kicking the falling stick. It hit Eailek in the face and while he dropped his stick to rub his face, I jumped on Gutax and head butted him in the face as we fell down and quickly punched Lohron and Tianshuk in the stomach when they swung their sticks. I grabbed the stick, hit Gutax again, and then hit both Lohron and Tianshuk at the same time, causing them to drop their sticks. I jumped up and back flipped away from the punch thrown at me and twirled around, hitting Berlox, Leidon, Eailek and the nameless vampire and then hit the other nameless vampire closest to me. I backed away and smiled at the ones that had managed to either stay on their feet or get back up.

Someone grabbed me from behind and, judging by the tingling sensation running up my arms, it was Shade. I had forgotten about him. One of the nameless grabbed the stick I was holding. He smiled before swinging it like a baseball bat. I just stared at it as it got closer to me and when it did, I quickly ducked, making it hit Shade in the chest. He loosened his hold on me with a groan while the other vampire swung again. He hit me in the back of the leg, hard. I went down on one knee and everyone laughed. Berlox grabbed my hair and pulled me to my feet. I let him do so, waiting for the right moment.

"See you aren't so hard," Lohron said, swinging his stick back.

"I wouldn't," I warned.

He just smiled. "What are you going to do about it?" His stick shot forward.

I spun around in Berlox's grip, making Lohron's stick skim my cheek. I lifted my leg up high and kicked him hard in the head before jumping up and wrapping my leg around his neck. I spun myself around fast and he flew across the room as I rolled to my feet. I ran forward and kicked the vampire holding the stick in the face before I grabbed it and swung it around fast, hitting Leidon, Gutax and Tianshuk hard. I snapped the bamboo stick in half with my knee before hitting Tianshuk hard once more. He flew backward with the force of it and crashed into Lohron, Eailek and both of the nameless vampires, knocking all over but one. I jumped forward and kicked one of the nameless vampires who managed to stay on his feet. As he crashed into the floor, I twisted around and hit Berlox and Leidon before back flipping, kicking Berlox, who had not bent over, in the face. I twisted around, hitting Tianshuk and Gutax, who were beside me when I landed on my feet.

I took a deep breath before looking at the groaning vampires on the floor. Then I looked at Shade, who was looking at me, impressed. I dropped the broken bamboo stick and walked toward him, watching him raise his eyebrows as he looked at the broken stick on the floor. I launched myself at him, knocked him to the floor and pinned him there.

"Lohron, you owe me a lot of money," Shade said, laughing.

I heard Lohron and the others groan. I smiled when Shade turned his attention onto me.

"You did not use my body against me."

"I forgot, too busy watching you move." He caught a lock of my hair in his hand and curled it around his hand. "You were amazing."

I could see the heat in his eyes, both from how close we were and from watching me fight. I felt much better now that I had had a good fight. I saw his eyes move, looking at my eyebrows, my eyes, my nose and then my lips before he pulled me to him. We were inches away when someone spoke from across the room.

"Layla."

I sat up and looked around. I smiled when I saw Nikalye.

"*Mi Belleza Oscura,* could I have a word please?" He spoke in Spanish.

I nodded and looked at Shade. "I will be back, he would like a word with me." He nodded and pushed me gently off him. I walked over to Nikalye and hooked my arm with his while we walked out of the hall and into the hallway. Nikalye spoke when we were out of earshot with everyone.

"You are okay?"

"I am, thank you. You?"

"I am fine." He looked at me curiously before speaking

again. "I have a request."

"What kind?" I asked, matching his curiosity.

"The kind you must take seriously," Nikalye replied.

"Okay, what is it?"

"If anything unusual happens between the two of you, you will let me know, yes?"

I tilted my head to the side, looking at Nikalye. "Unusual in what sense exactly?"

"You will know."

"You are not angry with me?"

"Until I know if I am correct in thinking what I am, no I am not."

"Okay. Yes I will tell you."

Nikalye smiled and kissed the top of my head. "Be careful."

"I will, Nikalye. Take care."

"Bye." Nikalye turned around and walked down the hall.

I watched him go until he had disappeared outside. The door behind me opened and Shade walked out with everyone following. I stepped to the side and watched them walk away, talking excitedly. I raised a questioning eyebrow at Shade.

"They've decided that they're going to throw a party before our next lesson," he answered.

I raised both of my eyebrows now. "You are going?"

He nodded. "I am."

"You are a bad influence, Mr. Shade."

He grinned with a flash of fangs. "You should come. Arezon wants you, too."

"I do not think so. I am not the type to party. Unless there will be fighting. I am not coming."

"Little Dhampir," Shade smiled at me. "One dance, if you do not want to stay, then I will let you go."

"One dance," I said, giving in to his luring voice.

"One dance," Shade reassured.

I looked away and considered. I did love dancing and it had been a long time since I had danced. I think I will enjoy dancing with Shade very much.

"Okay. One dance, that is all." Shade smiled and touched my arm gently, sending pleasure tingling up my arm. I looked at him up and down. I think dancing with Shade will be an experience I had never had, partly because of how we reacted when we touched. I was not going to be wearing many clothes when we danced.

Chapter Sixteen

Shade turned around when I stepped out of my lift a quarter of an hour later, his eyebrows rose fast. "There is not a lot to that dress."

"Are you complaining?" I asked.

He shook his head with a smile and his eyes were everywhere.

The front of the dress I chose was low, with a built in bra and a strip in the middle, under my breasts that went down my stomach, leaving my sides bare and connecting to the skirt, which flowed down to the middle of my thighs. The dress was backless, also leaving my back bare. There were thousands of tiny crystals covering the black material, making it sparkle when I moved. I gave Shade a twirl.

"Wow, I feel overdressed."

I laughed as I looked at his clothes. He looked very handsome in his dark blue shirt and light blue jeans. His long hair was wet, but he had somehow managed to do something with it. I think when it dried, it would make him look better.

"I take it you like the dress?" I asked. He pulled me to him, holding my hands to his chest.

"I love the dress."

I smiled while my heart raced and my body heated up. "Good, shall we go?" I asked as he bent to put his face into the curve of my neck.

"I don't know if you should ask me that. I'm all up for not going and taking that dress off you."

I laughed and shivered. "You asked me to come, Shade. I said one dance and you will get your one dance. I will not go back on that."

"If you dance as good as you look, then I'm going to have a good time."

I kept hold of his hand, despite my rising pleasure, and pulled him across the common room. I let Shade lead me when we got outside into the warm air as he knew where the party was. It did not take us long to get into the thick patch of trees. My pulse sped up to the same rhythm of the music as I neared it. I knew that the adults could hear all of this, but they did nothing.

There was a large clearing in the middle of the woods, a wide space with wood covering the floor, tables around it and teenage vampires dancing and chatting. The sky was in view, covered with stars that could be seen through the treetops.

No one noticed us when we walked into the clearing. I noticed Lohron and the others standing near some tables close to what I suspected was the dance floor, talking and drinking whatever was in their hands.

"Come, let us dance," I said, pulling Shade across the space, walking through the vampires and only stopping when we were in the middle, surrounded by them. I was aware that Shade's friends had seen us.

The music had changed now. It had a beat, yet it was slow and sexy at the same time. I turned in Shade's arms and began to move, swinging my hips from side to side slowly. I rubbed myself against him while doing so and raised my arms up in the air. I felt Shade's hands slide down my arms, leaving a pleasant tingling sensation, until his hands were on my bare hips. He moved from side to side with me. I let my arms and my head fall back on his shoulders as we moved up and down. The tingling sensation was getting stronger the more we rubbed against each other.

Shade gripped my hips tighter and I placed my own on top of his, still moving from side to side. I slowly moved down and he followed me before we moved back up again. I turned around and rubbed the full length of my body against his. I heard him suck in a breath and smiled with satisfaction. I ran my hands down his chest as I moved my hips from side to side. Shade gripped my hips tight once more, but I didn't stop moving. I moved my hips in a circular motion and felt his breath against my bare neck and shoulders. His hands roamed over my buttocks. He squeezed me gently before pulling me hard against him, leaving me almost breathless. Our faces were close now as we moved. I felt his hands slide up my back and opened my mouth as I turned my face up to the dark clear sky. I gasped with pleasure and raised my arms high above me once more before letting them slide over his head and then through his hair.

Shade lifted his hands up and laced his fingers through mine. He spun me around slowly so my back was to his chest again and held me tight against him.

"You are playing a dangerous game, Little Dhampir."

I smiled and turned my face toward his. "My middle name is dangerous." I rubbed harder against him and he sucked in another breath. He turned me quickly and pulled me to him. He nudged my head to the side and I felt his hot breath against my neck. I shivered and then moaned as pleasure shot through my entire body when he ran his hands up my bare back again and put his lips to my skin.

The song stopped and then changed to something faster. My pulse quickened to match the beat once more.

I stepped back from Shade. "One dance, that is all you

asked."

Shade smiled.

He knew I wanted to stay. I walked past him and off the dance floor. All eyes were on me as I passed. I walked back through the trees and out into the open space. I stopped for a second and took a deep breath before I walked into the common room. I did not lock my lift so it opened instantly for me. I was about to press the button to close the lift doors when I saw Shade walking toward me. I waited, my finger hovering over the button.

Before I could speak, he grabbed my arms and pushed me against the lift walls. He kissed me hard, slipping his tongue into my mouth, twisting it with my own. I moaned and heard the lift doors shut automatically. Shade stopped kissing me, ran his lips over my throat and nibbled on my sensitive skin. I closed my eyes as pleasure shot through me. I could do nothing but grip him against me tightly and gasp. He lifted his head and pressed the red button at the bottom of the panel. The doors locked.

He slipped his hands around me and lifted me up so I could wrap my legs around him. He pinned my body against the wall with his and kissed me again, slower this time. I moaned into his mouth and wrapped my legs tighter around him, pulling him further into me. I gasped when he ground himself against me. He was hard and he was rubbing the right places.

"Shade," I gasped his name when he pushed himself against me again. He growled slightly, obviously liking that. He shifted, putting me down on the floor before he ran his hands up my dress, his thumbs running along the inside of my thighs. I arched away from the floor as pleasure shot up my legs from where his hands were touching me. I moaned and gripped his arms tightly. If I was hurting him, he was not showing it.

He carefully pulled my panties down my legs and threw them in the corner. He resumed running his hands up my thighs. When he got close, I arched my back off the floor again as the pleasure pulsed through me. Shade kissed my cheek, then my lips when I turned my face to him and then slipped a finger into me. My pleasure exploded and I came.

I clenched my thighs around him, my cries lost against his lips as he kissed me hard. He held me on the floor with his free hand and his legs while he slid his finger in and out with the help of my wetness. When he added another one, I arched up, grabbing his moving hand with my own, making him stop.

"Ah, Little Dhampir cannot handle playing a dangerous game I see."

"This is not a dangerous game," I managed to gasp as I slid his fingers out of me and rubbed my aching clitoris with his slick fingers. His eyebrows rose, but he did not stop me. I closed my eyes and moaned as I my clitoris pulsed pleasure through the rest of my body. I felt my nipples harden and felt myself growing wetter the more I rubbed.

Shade growled, sensing my orgasm and when it came, I arched up, grabbing his thighs hard. He slipped two fingers into me. I cried out, my inner muscles clenching tight around him. I heard Shade groan. He moved his fingers fast while he rubbed my clitoris with his thumb. My eyes shot open with a gasp and I saw him watching me with heated eyes. I found that I could not look away as I cried out with pleasure again.

He slid his finger over my clitoris, making me arch up off the floor before he moved his hand away. My body was pulsing with mini shocks of my orgasm and my clitoris was throbbing when he slid his erection into me, stretching my inner walls and causing a moan to lock in my throat. I arched away from the floor once more as he filled me further. He leaned over me, putting his forehead against mine while I twitched, trying to control my breathing while my pleasure rose quickly.

"You're so tight, Little Dhampir." Shade growled against my lips.

It had been so long. He shifted and I moaned as he gripped my hips tight and pulled out slowly. He thrust himself in fast, slamming himself against me and pleasure shot through me when he slid back out and in, moving harder and faster.

My moans grew louder and louder while my body burned as if it was on fire. My pleasure exploded and I screamed, gripping Shade tight against me. He thrust himself harder into me, and I came in less than a second again. He brought me over the edge repeatedly.

Sweat dripped from both of our bodies, slightly burning me with each drop on my sensitive skin. I knew Shade wanted to give into his own pleasure, but he did not loosen the hold he had on me, and I did not want him to. He made me come once more before he could not stop his own pleasure from exploding. He slammed himself into me, buried his face in my neck and groaned with pleasure. I felt his heart racing along with my own as he sagged against me, trying to catch his breath. I tried to stay silent as he took a deep breath, taking my scent with him and letting it out slowly.

"Shade," I moaned his name when the pleasure inside rose instead of dying down. He lifted his head up and looked at me. He smiled before slowly sliding himself out.

"Beautiful," he murmured, watching my lips part as a moan escaped me.

"You have had experience," I said breathlessly as he pulled me to my feet. He kept hold of my arms, keeping the pleasure rising inside of me. If he did not stop touching me, I was going to come.

"How do you know?"

"An inexperienced person, human or vampire would never have taken me in a lift like you just did," I said as my eyes closed. I blew out a breath and took a step back. I looked him up and down. "An inexperienced person, human or vampire would never have been able to put on a condom and take me in the lift like you just did."

"Skill."

"That was more than skill," I told him. We both fell silent.

"I don't know what happened. I don't know why you react to my touch like you do every time I touch you."

I bent to pick my shorts up, remembering the first time he touched me, kissed me. Remembering how he reacted to my touch also. "It has never happened with previous lovers?"

"No. It has just been…normal." He looked at me up and down.

I could not help but shiver. There was something other than heat in his eyes, but I could not place it.

"This will complicate things when we train together."

"I highly doubt we will rip each other's clothes off when we train." Shade closed the space between us and pulled me against him hard, his hands splayed on my bare back. I gasped with pleasure before his mouth covered mine in a hungry kiss.

"We have to touch," he growled in a low voice, his lips still close to mine.

"We have done so before," I reminded him in a small voice. He kissed me once. "I felt the pleasure then, but not so much. It will be muted next time we fight." The look he gave me told me that he did not believe my words any more than I did. I did not care, I just didn't want him to stop kissing me.

"We shall see next time we get to fight."

Shade stepped away from me and pressed the button to the lift to open the doors. I made a small sound as he stepped out and put his hands either side to stop the doors from shutting.

"If I stay with you, Little Dhampir, we will miss our next lesson," Shade said, smiling.

I sighed. "It is good you don't want anyone knowing about us as much as me," I said, making him smile.

"Do not worry, this will not get around." He removed his hands and let the doors slide shut.

I saw him smile before the doors fully closed. I blew out a breath and leaned back against the wall as the lift took me up.

What had I gotten myself into?

Chapter Seventeen

Once I got into my room, I turned the shower on. I did not think I had enough time for a bath let alone a shower, and as much as I wanted to keep the scent of Shade on my skin, I knew the others would smell it easily. I let the water sooth my sensitive skin before I washed. When I stepped out, I headed straight for my wardrobe and dressed in black denim shorts, a white vest, and a grey checked shirt. After putting on some black canvas shoes, I tied my still curly hair up and headed for the lift.

Shade was waiting outside my lift when it opened. I was glad because I did not want us to ignore each other after what happened. I did not want us to ignore what happened because I could not. I could not ignore how he made me feel when he looked at me, when he spoke and when he touched me.

I could not ignore the rules, but whenever I looked at Shade, at the heat in the depths of his silver eyes, the love, all thoughts simply vanished.

When I stepped out of the lift, he took his time looking at me, looking at my tied up curly hair and my clothes.

"Little Dhampir," Shade greeted with a smile.

I smiled back and stepped forward. Shade did not move so I was very close to him now. "Shade," I replied. He put his face close to mine, but I turned my head away before he kissed me and whispered in his ear. "You cannot flirt with me, remember?" I stepped around him and smiled at him over my shoulder. He shook his head before following me out of the room and outside. Everyone was already in the hall when we walked in. When I saw Nikalye, I smiled widely and walked over to him.

"You are not guarding me, why?" I asked with amusement.

"You are making good progress, *mi Belleza Oscura*. I do not need to follow you around."

"I miss you."

Nikalye smiled. "And I miss you. Do not worry, I will always be here when I can. And you know you can see me whenever you want."

"I know, thank you, Nikalye."

"You do not need to thank me. I would do anything for you."

I hugged him. "Did you speak with Diaxon?" I asked into his chest.

"I did, you are going to be my example." He smiled and nodded, looking behind me.

I looked around at Diaxon just as he spoke.

"Okay, class. We are going to be trying something different this lesson. You will be fighting, but not in the usual way you are taught. I am going to let Master Nikalye teach you." He backed away and Nikalye stepped forward.

"Hello," he said, bowing his head. "I have a special ability that allows me to see the past, present and the future. The enemy cannot attack me if I know what their next attack is going to be and this is what I would like you all to try." He turned to me and gestured me forward. "Miss Layla here will give you an example of what I can do and then she will show you how she can pin me."

I took my shirt off and Diaxon held his hand out for it. Once I had given it to him, I walked into the middle of my hall and stretched. Nikalye took off his leather jacket and handed it to Diaxon. He stood in front of me and bowed at the waist.

I attacked and he twisted around, grabbing my arm and slamming me into the ground. I groaned as he stepped back. I did not expect him to pin me so quickly. I flipped myself to my feet and turned around, kicking out my leg. He grabbed it and closed his fingers around my throat. He turned around and threw me across the room. I turned in midair, landing swiftly on my feet. Nikalye was on me in a second, tripping me up. I swept my legs out, but he jumped over them and backed away. I pushed myself to my feet and walked toward him, running my fingers through my hair and tying it back up. When I got close enough, I punched him and then kicked out when he blocked it. He blocked that also before pushing me into the wall, hard, and then slamming me into the floor where he pinned me.

The room cheered loudly. Nikalye stood and pulled me to my feet and turned to the others once more while I rubbed the back of my head and walked into the middle of the hall.

"Miss Layla could not get a hit on me because her thoughts are not blocked. Now she will demonstrate her skills and she will be the one to pin me." Nikalye turned away from the disbelieving murmurs and motioned me to him.

I rolled my head on my shoulders before touching my toes. I walked forward and jumped in the air, sticking my left foot out. Nikalye blocked the attack, but I dropped to the floor and spun on my heels, knocking his feet out from underneath him. He fell to the floor, but rolled swiftly to his feet and kicked out. I back flipped quickly and then ran at Nikalye. He tried to grab me, but I twisted out of the way, wrapped my leg around his neck and spun around him, flipping him over. I jumped on him and pinned him.

"Good," Nikalye said as I got off him.

"There's no way we can do that!" Arezon said, looking at me in awe as everyone else murmured with agreement.

"There is an easier way to do it, if anyone has a bit of cloth."

Nikalye smiled and pulled a blindfold out of his pocket.

I took it from him while I shook my head. "You knew I was going to ask," I accused.

"I always know, *mi Belleza Oscura.*"

I smiled and put the blindfold on.

"If you cannot see Master Nikalye's attacks, then you do not need to think about how you are going to move, therefore—" Nikalye attacked before I finished. I sidestepped him and then kicked him in the back. "Nikalye does not know what your attack is going to be," I finished.

I ducked Nikalye's punch and then jumped back when he kicked. He circled me and I followed him with my fists in the air. He kicked again and I blocked it with my forearm before grabbing his arm and kneeing him in the stomach. I twisted around him and then flipped when my back was to his. I grabbed his neck, bringing him down hard and fast before I rolled backward, and swept his feet out from underneath him when he jumped to his feet. I pinned him. Some of the class cheered as I pulled my blindfold off and smiled at Nikalye.

"Layla is right, without her sight, she cannot see me attack and plan ahead. I am as blind as her."

I climbed off Nikalye and helped him to his feet. He turned to the others as I walked over to Diaxon to get my shirt.

"Well done, Layla."

I smiled and walked away, putting it back on.

"Okay, now I am not going to make you fight me because you do not have the experience like Layla has, but what I want you to do is get into pairs and one of you will be blindfolded. You have to anticipate your partner's moves and your partner has to anticipate your moves. I have blindfolds here."

Shade walked up to me and we smiled at each other.

"Do you think you can fight me, or do you want someone easier?" Shade asked.

I grinned. "Each other, even blindfolded, I can beat the others."

"Blindfolded and tied up, you can beat the others," Shade said as he took the blindfold out of my hands.

Our fingers touched and our gazes locked. A slight tingling sensation travelled through my fingers and I knew Shade was as affected as I was.

"Okay, ladies and gentlemen."

Shade and I stepped away from each other and looked at Nikalye who was rounding everyone into the middle of the hall. I cast a glance at Shade and then walked to the others. Shade stood close behind me when I stopped, I could feel the heat coming off him.

"Because some of you are going to be blindfolded, Diaxon will be taking some of you into the other hall so you do not hurt each other. I want you to try hard at this, because if you can sense the enemies, you can beat them without getting hurt. This is very important." Nikalye moved half of the pairs to one side and Diaxon took them out of the hall, into the other one.

I moved away once more, into the space at the bottom of the hall. Shade put on his blindfold and I circled him, staying very close to him. He grabbed me and pushed me into the wall.

"You know this is kind of kinky."

I laughed. "How is it?" I ran my hands up his top. He growled quietly and pushed himself into me.

"Being blindfolded, I have to feel my way around," he emphasised his words by running his hands down my collarbone and over my breasts.

I could feel the pleasure from his hands through my top.

"Ah, so you do." I gasped. I dropped down to the floor and tripped him up. I pinned him. "But you cannot distract me."

Shade laughed. "Well I see that I can't now. I guess I will have to—" he flipped me over and pinned me— "try again."

I pulled my hands out of his grip and hit him.

He laughed.

"You can't do that."

"Why can't I?" he asked, putting his lips close to mine.

"Because you can't distract a human with your charm."

Shade moved his face away from mine slightly. "Yeah okay, good point."

I laughed and pushed him off me. I saw Nikalye shake his head at us before turning away to assist someone else.

Shade moved quickly, tripping me. I flipped myself up, kicking him in the face before spinning and kicking the side of his face. I jumped on his back and pinned his hands above his head.

"*Mi Belleza Oscura*, maybe you should be the one to be blindfolded," Nikalye called from across the room.

I climbed off Shade, but he swept his feet out, knocking me to the floor. He pinned me and everyone cheered. Shade pulled off his blindfold and climbed off me. I blew out a breath before taking his outstretched hand and getting to my feet. Shade put the blindfold on me and then kissed me. I spun around and hooked my leg around his. I pinned him to the floor.

"You cannot distract me," I said before climbing off him.

"I can try." Shade laughed.

I pulled my blindfold up. He put his arm around my

shoulder. I looked around the hall. Everyone in the room was very good I had to admit. However, no one was moving fast and only seemed to be attacking when their partners were distracted.

I felt Shade's fingers on my shoulder and then down my arm. I looked up at him and he smiled before raising his eyebrows.

"*Mi Belleza Oscura.*"

I looked at Nikalye and saw him gesturing me over. I looked at Shade and he shrugged. I walked over to Nikalye and he pulled the blindfold down carefully.

"You have much experience with this, try something else."

I sensed him turning to the others.

"Remember when I said to you that if you should all run at me and attack me, I can put you on the floor?"

Everyone chorused yes.

"I told you that it has nothing to do with the fact that I am a trained guard, it is because you did not plan. What I want you to do is plan your attacks, work together and see if you can pin Miss Layla to the floor. Shade, step to the side, I do not think it is wise for you to join in."

Shade chuckled and move away from me.

"Relax, clear your mind and breathe. Remember what you were taught," Nikalye spoke in Spanish so the others could not understand as he retreated.

I breathed in deeply and then blew it out, relaxing my mind and blocking out all the sounds except for the vampires around me. Everything went quiet and then I heard a rustle of clothes. I shifted to the side and bent forward and lifted my leg up, kicking the vampire in the head. Once my foot was on the ground, I dropped down and then jumped back.

Everything went silent again. I shifted my foot, sliding it

along the floor before jumping in the air and spinning, kicking a vampire. I back flipped, kicking someone else. I punched someone and then spun, punching another three before dropping down to the floor with my left leg bent and my right leg sticking out to the side. I took another deep calming breath.

The door opened and I straighten up as the other group walked into the hall.

I back flipped quickly before jumping into the air and kicking both my feet out to the side. As soon as I landed, I dropped to the floor and swept their feet out, knocking them to the floor. I stood and blocked a punch with my forearm before grabbing it and spinning around, launching the vampire across the room. From the grunts and groans, I had knocked others over.

I lifted my foot up high in front of me before bending forward, lifting my foot up behind me, kicking the vampire in front and behind. I kicked someone with both feet before flipping myself up and backing away. I spun around and kicked out, but someone ducked that and grabbed me from behind. I pushed back as he loosened his grip on me. I ran forward and ran up the wall before back flipping. When I landed on the floor, everything was quiet once more.

I could hear a couple of vampires moving around me, but none attacked. I took a deep breath and blew it out slowly before I stepped forward and lifted my leg up high, kicking someone in the face. I bent forward and twisted around with my hand on the floor, kicking someone else. I straightened and then ducked and twisted around on the floor with my leg stuck out before I quickly jumped up and spun. The vampire ducked quickly before knocking my legs out from underneath me. As I fell he jumped on me and pinned my hands above my head.

The room erupted into loud cheers and applause.

"I knew it would be you to knock me down," I said. Shade laughed and pushed himself off me. He pulled me to my feet and I took my blindfold off.

"They were never going to pin you," Shade said as Nikalye walked up.

"Well done, Shade. You see." He turned to the cheering class and they quietened down. "You all did not work together when attacking Layla, but when you knew you were not going to knock her down, you decided to talk. If you continue to teach yourself how to plan, you will find it easier to fight." He smiled at me when Diaxon spoke.

"Okay, now this lesson is almost over—"

Everyone groaned.

"But if you wish to begin your next training lesson, I have no problem with that. I will just move the other session to later, but you all need to feed first. You have an hour to do so."

Everyone began to talk in excited voices as they walked across the room.

Shade touched my arm gently, making me look at him.

"Are you coming or—"

"I am going to say goodbye to Nikalye. I will see you next lesson," I told him, smiling. He nodded and stroked my cheek before walking across the room. I watched him leave and then turned to Nikalye. "You do have to leave, do you not?"

He bowed his head. "I wish I could stay, but I cannot."

"Is Father coming?" I asked.

"He is, but you will not see him until later on."

I nodded, suddenly feeling happier. I walked across the room, following Nikalye.

Chapter Eighteen

"Some of you have made a request to learn how to fight with these," Diaxon held up a bamboo stick.

I smiled widely as everyone murmured to each other. After my fight with the others, it was not surprising that some wanted to learn how wield the weapon.

"So we will be working in pairs once more. You may choose your own. When you have done so, please collect your weapons."

Shade walked across the hall, followed by some others while I stayed where I was, watching him go with a smile. When I had my weapon, I smiled as everyone stood spaced out so they did not hit anyone around them with their sticks.

"Okay, stand in your positions and strike out. Don't forget to block as well as hit," Diaxon said.

Shade set his feet apart and I did the same. I held my stick exactly how I always held it. Shade held his in the middle so that his hands touched each other. He touched his with mine and then we both swung. He swung low, I swung high. I blocked his spear with mine and managed to hit him in the shoulder at the same time. He moved back a couple of steps. I smiled.

"Well done, Layla, Diaxon said loudly. "See what she did? She watched not only his stick, but his body also. Something Shade forgot to do. Everyone try it."

I took my left hand off the stick and swung it in my right

hand in a figure of eight motion, going from side to side. I did it quickly and noticed that no one was attacking each other, they were looking at me with amazement.

Shade tracked me, but I was moving too fast for his eyes to see. When the stick was on the right side of my body, I grabbed it with my left hand and swung it fast. I knocked his legs from underneath him and pointed the end to his neck. The room gasped and I heard someone — Lohron no doubt — make a noise of disbelief. I was a dhampir after all and I should not be able to move so quickly.

"How do you move that fast?" he asked with his hands in the air above him. He was not a sore loser, he was genuinely amazed with my skill.

I removed the stick and held it out. He grabbed it and I pulled him to his feet.

"I taught myself how to use a weapon similar to this." I did not tell him that after teaching myself, I had fought strong vampires and Spirit Demons. I was having too much fun.

We started again. This time, while I swirled the stick in my hands, everyone was paying attention, watching my movements. Shade tracked my moves easily, so when I swung, he blocked it effortlessly.

He just did not block the other end I swung. It hit him in the back, but he brushed it off like a fly. I turned around so I could have speed on my side and twisted the spear above my head. When I swung it, Shade moved his high to block it again, but just before our spears hit, I kicked up high, knocking his out of his hands. My stick hit him in the shoulder and I once again twisted around and hit him behind the knees. He fell to the floor again.

"Damn. I'm no match against you when you use strategy against me," he said as some of the vampires clapped, not caring that they were cheering on a dhampir. I laughed as I helped him to his feet again.

"That is why we are here, is it not? To learn to fight in all forms."

Shade smiled as he walked away to get his spear. He stood in front of me and swung his stick around fast. I blocked it and let him swing again, this time lower. I jumped and was about to swing my own stick when I stopped.

I could not explain what made me do such a foolish thing, but I knew something wasn't right. Shade obviously sensed nothing, he swung at me, but I grabbed hold of his hand to stop him and then put my hand on his chest to keep him still. I was looking at the door, where the footsteps were getting louder as they got closer.

"What?" Shade asked. His voice was loud in the very quiet room.

I did not answer his question straight away because I did not know who it was. All I knew was that it was not good at all. Shade opened his mouth, but I interrupted him. "I have this uneasy feeling. Something is going to happen."

"Are you serious?"

The door opened and six tall men dressed in white strode into the room, three on the left, and the other three on the right. They stood straight-backed with their hands clasped in front of them. They all had three headed swords criss-crossing their backs.

A woman with long wavy black hair, a pale face and blue eyes strode into the room. She stopped and surveyed everything. She was wearing white flared trousers and a white top that hung over her shoulders. The sleeves were long with a slit starting from her shoulders, to her wrists. Her eyes met mine and when she smiled, it was an evil smile.

"Mother—" I said it in disbelief because it could not be my mother. My mother was dead.

"Layla, how nice to see you again." She smiled.

I raised my stick up fast, blocking the two swords I had sensed. Something invisible pushed Shade aside and he skidded across the floor until he hit the wall. He got up fast as I ducked the sword and I saw him walking forward. The six guards were in front of Shade and the others before he could walk any further. An invisible force pushed everyone in the hall against the wall. They obviously tried to struggle, but against Spirit Demons, it was useless. I saw that Diaxon did not. He had obviously encountered Spirit Demons before. The guards pulled out their weapons. I knew the threat well, anyone who came to my aid would die.

I lifted one end of my stick up, blocking the sword and swung the other end around. I felt the impact on the stick. I felt it stagger back, but then recover quickly. When the swords were swinging at me again, I blocked each blow while I moved backward. When my back hit the wall, I ducked quickly and felt the vibration through the wall as both swords sunk into the stone.

I moved away and looked at Mother.

She was standing tall with her eyes on me, watching my every move as the Spirit Demon attacked me. I looked back and watched the swords come out of the wall. They moved in a circle, one after the other, as though the person holding them was twisting their wrist, making a figure of eight motion.

The swords moved faster while getting closer to me. I could follow the rhythm easily. The swords swung out fast and I moved to the side, but not fast enough. One of the swords sliced through my top and into my skin. I bent backward when the other sword swung toward my neck. I heard the whistle of the blade. I put my hands onto the floor and lifted myself up. I kicked it in the face before I landed back on my feet. I lifted the stick up and once again, I was blocking the hits. I twisted the stick in my hands and then swung it fast. One of the swords flew across the room. The other one cut into my shoulder deeply.

I cried out with pain and anger. My vision went red before I turned to put distance between me and the sword. My stick was knocked out of my hand as I ran toward the wall. It flew high behind me and I heard the Spirit Demon behind me, the sword outstretched. If I turned back now, I would die.

I continued to run opposite where my spear was flying and ran up the wall when I got to it. I felt the sting of silver against my skin, but did not stop. I took three steps before I pushed myself backward. When I landed on the floor, I back flipped, narrowly avoiding the sword as it swung, missing my stomach. I back flipped fast, four times before I jumped up high. I caught the stick in my hands and landed on my feet. I skidded backward because of the force. When I stopped, I swung the stick instantly. The sword was swinging too strong and one sword knocked my hand that was holding the stick. Then I felt the burn of silver as the sword stabbed into my right thigh. I fell to my knees as blood gushed out of my open wound, a small gasp leaving me.

I felt the presence behind me and then I was suddenly rising with the stick in my hands as it lifted up. I pulled against it as it moved toward my throat, but I was not strong enough, especially with my injured shoulder.

I fought to get the stick away from me. I could not breathe. Vampires could hold their breath for a long period, but forcing it out of me stopped me from being able to hold my breath. I was suffocating. I closed my eyes, but could not concentrate on anything. The sound of my heart beating was too loud in my ears. I tried to breathe, but it was no use.

Slowly, my whole body started to go numb. I felt my

heavy arms drop to my sides where they swung uselessly. I felt my legs buckle, but I did not fall. The stick around my neck kept me up.

There was a roar on the other side of the room. A door was smashed open and then I felt the floor underneath me. I breathed in and out and coughed. My heartbeat was fast, getting the blood circulating through my body once more. Pain burst in my head like lightning as the blood rushed to my brain. I found myself wanting to be sick. I did not though. I pushed myself up onto my knees and looked around. The room spun and I had to shut my eyes for a couple of seconds before opening them.

I saw Tyroz, Nikalye, Shifter, Diaxon and Doxiak standing by the teenage vampires. Asking them what happened. The guards seen with Mother had gone. Shade was by my side. His tingling touch calmed me down as he helped me to my feet. I winced with pain and leaned against him when I felt myself falling back down.

"Little Dhampir."

I did not speak, just looked up at Mother. She was up against the wall with both of her hands were pinned above her head by a large one. Another hand was around her throat, strangling her. The man that held her was tall. His hair was pitch black, like Mother's, tied in a ponytail at the back of his head. He wore black clothes and he was extremely angry.

It is Riyzan Theraux—the oldest living vampire in existence.

About the Author

I was born in Plymouth Devon and moved to Lincoln at a young age. I have been to University of Lincoln, Riseholme College, studying a course on Animal Care, which I did for two years. I now live with my boyfriend, Reece, and our little zoo, which includes; my hamster named Crunch, a chinchilla called Hektor and three guinea pigs, Fluff, Smudge and Squig.

We both love animals and hope to have an army of guinea pigs, hamsters and chinchilla's. Along with a goat.

I miss my other hamster, Hamster, aka Scratch, and love him loads. I miss his squeak chats over tea.

Since I was fourteen, I have written various books until I came up with the idea of Eternal Darkness in the Cursed in Darkness Series.